W9-BHM-471

"The Cult of Diablos... That's our enemy."

Well...it's not like they actually exist.

be one of them.
Think of children who worship their favorite superheroes.
That was me but with master puppeteers.
Nu
Beta
Gamma
"We lurk in the darkness and hunt down shadows..."

Delta
Shadow
“We are the Shadow Garden…”
Alpha

PLEE
EEEE
EEEE
EEE
GH!!!”
Rose
Oriana
The Eminence

"Hidden Normie Technique: Spinning Guard, Bloody Tornado!"
Cid Kagenou
The Eminence

Claire Kagenou
The Eminence
Rose Oriana
The Eminence
"Since you've saved my life...I shall give my heart to you."
"Um... I baked you cookies."
Sherry Barnett
The Eminence

"My little brother's a cheeky one… which is why I make life hard for him."
"Your swordplay isn't bad…but I don't like it."
Alexia Midgar
The Eminence

THE
Eminence
IN
Shado

01

The Eminence in Shadow

01

Daisuke Aizawa

Illustration by
Touzai

New York

THE Eminence IN Shadow 01

DAISUKE AIZAWA

Translation by Kristi Fernandez
Cover art by Touzai

Yen On
150 West 30th Street, 19th Floor
New York, NY 10001

Visit us at yenpress.com ▪ facebook.com/yenpress ▪ twitter.com/yenpress
yenpress.tumblr.com ▪ instagram.com/yenpress

First Yen On Edition: July 2020

Library of Congress Cataloging-in-Publication Data
Names: Aizawa, Daisuke, author. | Touzai, illustrator. | Fernandez, Kristi, 1992– translator.
Title: The eminence in shadow / Daisuke Aizawa ; illustration by Touzai ;
translation by Kristi Fernandez ; cover art by Touzai.
Other titles: Kage no jitsuryokusha ni naritakute. English
Description: First Yen On edition. | New York, NY : Yen On, 2020.
Identifiers: LCCN 2019034416 | ISBN 9781975359058 (v. 1 ; hardcover)
Subjects: CYAC: Secret societies—Fiction. | Good and evil—Fiction. | Fantasy.
Classification: LCC PZ7.1.A369 Em 2019 | DDC [Fic]—dc23
LC record available at https://lccn.loc.gov/2019034416

ISBNs: 978-1-9753-5905-8 (hardcover)
978-1-9753-5906-5 (ebook)

10 9 8 7 6 5 4 3 2 1

LSC-C

Printed in the United States of America

The Eminence in Shadow

The Eminence in Shadow

nestly can't remember what catalyzed this desire.

l know is I've admired shadowbrokers for as long as
n remember.

s it a certain anime? Or was it a manga—or a movie?

I guess it doesn't matter. I was all in for anything that featured a
stermind, or an eminence in shadow, as I like to call them. These
racters were never the protagonists or final bosses but were relegated to a role
ind the scenes where they flaunted their powers and meddled in the
irs of others. I've always looked up to the men in the shadows.

anted to be one of them.

All I know is I've admired shadowbrokers for as long as
I can remember.

Was it a certain anime? Or was it a manga—or a movie?

Eh, I guess it doesn't matter. I was all in for anything that featured a
mastermind, or an eminence in shadow, as I like to call them. These
characters were never the protagonists or final bosses but were relegated to a role
behind the scenes where they flaunted their powers and meddled in the
affairs of others. I've always looked up to the men in the shadows.

I wanted to be one of them.

Think of children who worship their favorite superheroes.

That was me, but with master puppeteers.

Preparing the Perfect Stage!

Prologue

The Eminence in Shadow

Prologue

I honestly can't remember what catalyzed this desire. All I know is I've admired shadowbrokers for as long as I can remember.

Was it a certain anime? Or was it a manga—or a movie? Eh, I guess it doesn't matter. I was all in for anything that featured a mastermind, or an eminence in shadow as I like to call them. These characters were never the protagonists or final bosses but were relegated to a role behind the scenes where they flaunted their powers and meddled in the affairs of others. I've always looked up to the men in the shadows. I wanted to be one of them.

Think of children who worship their favorite superheroes. That was me but with master puppeteers.

Well, there was one thing that set us apart: My reverence for them wasn't short-lived. In fact, it buried itself deeper in my heart, never dying out and always guiding me through life. To become stronger, I learned everything from karate to boxing, from swordplay to mixed martial arts. I hammed it up during all my practices, concealing my true power from the world and preparing for the fated day.

At school, I played the part of being pleasantly mediocre, an unassuming face in the crowd. Like an NPC in a game or a part of the mob. I didn't do any harm. But behind this facade of normalcy, I was training full throttle. That's how I spent my entire youth.

But as time passed, an uneasy feeling started to haunt me: I was due for a reality check.

Yeah, that's right.

This was all for nothing.

I realized I'd never become as powerful as shadow commanders in the stories. It didn't matter how hard I trained in martial arts. Sure, I could clobber a few punks...but that was it. It'd be a tough fight if anyone drew a gun, and if I was surrounded by soldiers in full gear, I'd be toast, donezo, old news.

The idea of a shadowbroker getting curb stomped by some soldiers... Ha! Ridiculous! Let's say I trained for ten more years—or that I became the greatest martial artist in the world. I'd still get rekt by a gang of commandos.

Or maybe I'd manage to escape by the skin of my teeth or train hard enough to fight back. It's all in the realm of possibility. But even if I somehow managed to do that, these guys could set off a nuke and vaporize me in an instant. There is a limit to the human body. That much I know.

That said, my master puppeteers would never be taken down by a nuke. Which means I needed to be impervious to them, too.

What does one need to survive a nuclear attack?

Is it the ability to pack a punch?

Could it be a body of steel?

How about unlimited stamina?

Wrong, wrong, and wrong again. You need a totally different kind of power.

Some call it magic. Others, mana. Or chi, or aura, or...you get the point. Anything will do. I needed to obtain this clandestine ability. I'd managed to reach this conclusion when I finally confronted reality head-on.

I'll try to explain. Let's say someone is on a quest for magical powers. Anyone would think they're nuts. Hell, I know I would. I'd think they'd gone bonkers.

But consider this: No one in the world has proved that magic exists—or disproved it.

I couldn't find these powers with my sanity intact. I had to dive to the depths of lunacy.

*   *   *

I started training in a new way that was damn near impossible.

After all, no one knows how to acquire magic, mana, chi, auras, or what have you.

I practiced Zen meditation; I braved the purification ceremony of standing under waterfalls; I focused my entire being inward; I fasted; I mastered the art of yoga; I converted religions; I searched for holy spirits; I prayed to god; I strapped myself to a cross. There was no right answer, which meant I groped my way through the darkness and sprinted down my chosen path.

Which brings us here. I'm just about ready to start my final summer as a high schooler, and I've yet to discover magic or mana or chi or auras…

It is already dark by the time I finish my daily training session.

I pick up and put on my underwear, which I'd chucked to the side, and wiggle my arms through the sleeves of my school uniform. I have yet to pick up these secret magical skills, but I've been starting to feel the effects of my training, I think, of late.

Like right now.

I can see flashing lights going off in my mind and sense the world is spinning.

It could be magic…or auras… In either case, I'm feeling its effects—that's for sure. I'm proud to announce that I've completed another successful session.

When I'm in the thick of it, I rip off every single article of clothing and get buck naked in the forest. It makes me one with the universe. I bash my skull into the trunk of a giant tree to physically force out my worldly thoughts. Plus, it stimulates my brain and urges my latent powers to awaken.

You know, I'm all about logic when it comes to these things.

Yeah, everything's beginning to get all blurry right about now. It's a sensation comparable to giving myself a concussion. I make my way out of the forest with the lightest of footsteps, feeling like I'm treading on clouds.

Just then, I see light—two beams floating in the air and slicing through space. How strange. They're beckoning me, guiding me somewhere.

"Ma-magic…?" I whisper, tiptoeing toward the illumination.

It must be… It's gotta be! I finally found the powers of the unknown!

I notice that I've gone from walking to sprinting, tripping over the roots of trees and continuing to stagger forward—on and on like a beast in the forest.

"Magic! Magic! Magic! MAGIC, MAGIC, MAGIC!!!!!" I chant, bounding toward the lights and ready to snatch them out of midair…

"Hmm…?"

As a pair of headlights flood my vision with a blinding whiteness, I hear the shrill whine of a sudden brake ringing and ringing.

And then a collision. Its impact pierces through my body… And my magic…

In conclusion, I was able to find magical powers.

When I open my eyes, I sense that I'm surrounded by its energy, though I gotta admit it looks different from the two lights. Eh, no biggie.

Oh, and one other small detail: As a side effect, I manage to reincarnate. I bet I opened a door to another world when I found magic or something. Whatever.

As for right now, I'm a baby boy, a few months old. I only recently started forming thoughts, but it's still hard for me to guess how much time has elapsed at any given moment. Plus, I don't know any words, but I guess it's plenty to recognize that this civilization is more or less the same as Europe in the Middle Ages.

But none of that's important. I've acquired magical powers. That's the end-all be-all. I couldn't care less about how it happened or any bonus features.

I notice magic as soon as I start displaying glimmers of consciousness. All around me, I can see minuscule grains of light floating and shimmering. It reminds me of those times in my past life when I frolicked through a field of flowers stark naked—to train and find spirits, obviously.

As it turns out, my training wasn't a total waste after all. I mean, my ability to detect this energy is proof enough, and I can control it as easily as my limbs. It's comparable to when I strapped my naked body to a cross, a nod to Jesus...or maybe when I flip-flopped religions and danced around in prayer in my birthday suit... I bet every little thing in my training sessions helped me in the long run. It's already taught me that I can get stronger.

Plus, time is of no consequence for a baby. I'm ready to use these years to train and become an eminence in shadow, once and for all... Oops, I think I've made a doodie.

Which reminds me. I heard somewhere that birds let their droppings dribble out involuntarily, and I think human babies are the same. I can fight the good fight with logic and reasoning, but it feels as though my instincts take over, whispering *Just do it* in my ear.

That said, this is me we're talking about. I spent my waking hours training in my past life. Pooling together all the strength in my body, I tighten my sphincter, buying me some time...

"Wwwaaaahhhhh!"

...to summon people.

I think it's been ten years.

You know, magic is something else. It means I can surpass the bodily limitations of humans: lift ginormous boulders with a single finger, dash twice as fast as a horse, leap higher than a house.

That said, I'm no match for nukes. Well, I know my defenses will increase with my magical capacity, but have you *seen* the firepower of those weapons on Earth? There was a time when I contemplated forgetting about them entirely, 'cause we don't have nukes in this world.

But what good is a master puppeteer who settles for less?

No good. Not at all.

That means my next mission is to become strong enough to beat weapons of mass destruction. After extensive research and training, I found one potential solution, which I've been incorporating into my daily experiments.

Oh yeah. And it seems I've been born into a noble family. For generations, members of this family have trained to become dark knights, who use magic to power up and slay enemies in battle. And as my family's rising star of a son (...*NOT*), I'm living my days as your average apprentice. After all, shadowbrokers need to be extremely selective about when, where, and to whom they reveal their powers. Yeah...I'll lie in wait until then.

I know I'm not exerting my true potential and that I am cutting corners, but I learned some skills as an apprentice that have come in handy. Like how magic is used on the battlefield in this world. It's been a good opportunity for me to reflect on my own techniques.

To be completely honest, it's clear to me the fighting styles from my past life were a hundred times more logical and refined than the ones here. I mean, look at any contemporary martial arts battle. These fighters rebuke unnecessary movements, drawing from various combat schools and whittling them down to the crème de la crème. This creates the conditions for the "perfect" fight. It relies on the rules of the game, of course, but this mental attitude can be used to identify the best of the best in any situation.

And then consider this world. First and foremost, their fighting techniques stay in their country of origin. Which means different schools of combat don't cross borders. Plus, there are certain secret skills that countries won't allow out of their jurisdiction—not that we'd be able to spread them to begin with, since no forms of media are readily available to us. This means we can't combine techniques from other forms of fighting, much less reject or improve our own.

If I had to describe this system in one word, I'd call it *unrefined.*

But there's one fundamental difference between the two worlds. That's right: magic. It completely changes the baseline of physical performance.

Take physical strength, for example.

I can lift someone up with one hand, which means any knowledge about hand-to-hand combat and wrestling, or "ground fighting," goes out the window. Even if we're in a mounted grappling position, I can soar through the air by flexing my abs. If I've got my foot hooked on an opponent in an offensive guard, I can blast them off me by activating my leg muscles. Yeah. Ground fighting is out of the question.

It's like how humans have their method of combat and gorillas have a breed of their own. And I'll just leave it at that.

There are also differences in the distance and speed at which combatants step into their attacks—meaning it's harder to predict their movements in battle. This might be the most important thing. I mean, martial arts are all about reading your opponent at an appropriate range. The angle, position, and distance of your attacks are everything.

It took me a while to get the hang of the last one, especially because these fighters attack from afar. Like sixteen feet apart. I mean, I guess I get it. They're lightning fast and take ginormous steps, and I'd just assumed this was their way of fighting…until I realized it was to compensate for their poor defense tactics.

I'm sure this is relatable to all martial artists: Those who can't guard will stand too far from their opponents.

It's really scary to get hit. I get it. It's tempting to retreat to where your opponent can't reach you. But this results in a contest where one fighter attacks and the other retreats, and vice versa, which is a real snore. You call this outboxing? Try again. This is just an exercise of running back and forth.

It doesn't matter if the fighters are five or a hundred meters apart.

They can't land a decent hit either way. It could be six or seven or ten meters—it's all the same.

This has been a public service announcement to close the gap and duke it out.

But once you cross a certain threshold, one millimeter can make a huge difference. And it stands at the exact point where I can both land a blow and react to an attack. Throw in other factors like the angle of my hits, and the slightest turn can mean an advantage—or a disadvantage. The narrowest of margins is the best range between two fighters.

A battle shouldn't be about one combatant dashing in sixteen feet and the other leaping back nineteen.

I guess I came into this whole thing with an idea of what to expect from other worlds, which—compounded with my unfamiliarity with magic—left me confused about their combat scene. But, eh, I've gotten my bearings straight as of late. It's all chill now.

I train every day at home, where our dad basically directs us on how to throw down, and I grapple with my older sister. I know she's only two years older than me, but she has natural talent, according to everyone else. If she keeps it up, she's the one who will take over as head of the family, which isn't uncommon in this world, since magic can make women powerful enough to become the heir.

"Geez, you're so strong...," I whimper every day as she kicks my ass.

But I can't win. If I want to become a shadow commander, I've got to establish myself as the most average of all background characters.

That's how I've been living out my day-to-day. Tack on lessons about how to act as an aristocrat and hanging out with people to secure my place as a low-profile extra, and I've barely got any free time during the day.

Which means the only time for me to train is after everyone else has gone to bed, late into the night. I may be cutting into my beauty sleep, but I've been using magic to recover super-quick and meditation to catch some *z*'s in new ways. And now, I've pretty much got short sleeper syndrome. I make it work.

Okay, time to get down to business. I blast through my usual training regimen in the forest. I've got something special planned today.

I heard that rogues have taken up residence in the ghost town nearby. According to my investigation, it's a large gang of thieves—and the perfect opportunity to test my new weapon.

I take down bandits here and there. But a whole group of criminals? That's the event of the year. And I'm always short on sparring partners, so I welcome evildoers with open arms.

Oh, please, please, please infest this place with more crime!

I think it's standard for villages to try to deal with offenders on their own terms, but they mostly get away scot-free. I mean, our judicial system is in the city, which is why I've decided to take the law into my own hands.

Today marks the historic day of my first official battle with my newest weapon. I've been experimenting with it for months and call it the "slime bodysuit."

Allow me to explain.

We can use magic in this world to strengthen our bodies and weapons, but there are energy losses when it's transferred from one form to another. For example, if I run one hundred currents of magic through an average steel sword, only 10 percent of them will be of use in combat. A whopping 90 percent is lost. Even a mithril sword, which is known to be compatible with magic. It's considered high-end if it performs at 50 percent capacity.

That's when slimes caught my eye. A slime is a magical being that uses energy to change form and wobble from place to place. According to my research, I've found they have a conductivity of an astonishing 99 percent. On top of that, they're in a liquid state, which means they can change their shape at will.

I started testing slime jellies after capturing and crushing their cores—easily more than a thousand of them. In fact, I pushed them to the brink of extinction in my area by killing too many and had to go on an expedition to find more.

The jellies are easy to handle and strong, to boot. I successfully molded the slime into a wearable bodysuit, which is super-lightweight and silent, unlike armor. Plus, it almost, like, supports my movements? And I've given it killer defenses, of course.

As for right now, I'm wrapped in a black slime bodysuit. It's a simple, no-frills getup that fits my body perfectly, except for eyes, nostrils, and mouth. I'm virtually indistinguishable from the criminal in a certain famous detective manga.

I might want to think up a more suitable design when I'm intervening in a scheme as a full-fledged shadowbroker.

I manage to arrive at the ghost town late into the night, but I can see a few lights in the darkness. The thieves seem to be having a feast to celebrate their robbing of merchants. Wow, I'm super-lucky.

You see, thieves aren't good at planning, and they immediately squander what they steal, which means they only have something decent right after a successful attack. And one man's treasure is another man's treasure. What's theirs is mine. This is how I'll get the funds to become a puppet master.

Anyway, I crash their feast, excited as all hell—not with a surprise attack, because that won't make for a good practice session.

"Yahoo! Hand over the loot, scumbags!" I shriek in the middle of their banquet.

"Wh-who the hell is this puny dude?!"

I mean, I'm only ten years old. Like, duh. It's only natural that I'm short.

"You heard me! Now fork over the goods!" I shout, punting the rude man across the room for calling me small.

The other thieves finally draw their weapons.

"Hey, keep it up, and we ain't gonna hold back, you bra—…!"

"Take that!" I exclaim as I slice through his neck, severing his head from his shoulders midsentence.

That's right. My sword is made of slime, which means I can draw it from my bodysuit when the situation calls for it. And it has a bunch of nifty functions.

Number one. It can elongate.

"Take that! And that! And that!" I extend my sword and slay all the dinky thieves in the vicinity.

I stretch the slime out in the shape of a whip with edges as sharp as a sword. It's my first time wielding it, so I'm a tad nervous, but I can totally see how it might come in handy.

"And that! And that! And…huh?"

I notice the room has gone all silent as I get a little too carried away with slashing and slicing around me.

Wait, is there only one guy left?

"Wh-who are you…?"

"Eh, I guess you'll be my guinea pig for function number two."

"Th-the hell do you mean…?!"

"To break it down, you look stronger than the rest of them. I'm assuming you're like their boss or something, right? Your chances of winning are squat, but if you let me practice on you, I bet you'll live for, like, two extra minutes. Good luck."

"S-stop playing, you brat! In the capital, I'm the—…!"

"Hey, you. Skip the speech and come at me."

"Die, dammit!" booms the Boss (or whatever) as he closes the distance between us, taking his sweet old time to swing at me, and I obviously… don't budge.

His sword plunges straight into my chest, and I'm thrown to the ground on impact.

"Ha-ha! That's what you get for messin' with me! I've mastered the Royal Bushin method, and… Wh-what?!"

"Ta-daa! …You couldn't even scratch me."

I rise to my feet as if nothing happened, and wow, I couldn't be happier with my suit's defenses! I mean, these weak-as-shit attacks can't even touch me.

"I've heard it seems to be all the rage in the capital. Show me."

"Damn you!" swears the Boss as he strikes me.

Yeah. No sweat. As he swings his sword with all his might, I don't even ready mine, sidestepping and ducking to dodge him, no problem.

The Royal Bushin method, was it? I could get into their ways of wielding the sword.

I mean, it's not every day you get to see someone fighting over something other than spirituality, old-fashioned standards, or personal beliefs in this world. This was a fight motivated by logic. I can see it from his clumsy set of attacks.

In the length of a second, a small step forward.

I see him calculate his next strike and take creative approaches. That said, his attacks leave a lot to be desired, and in the next free moment, I step just out of his range.

"Wh-why...why can't I hit you?!"

"I mean, you're weaker than my old man. Though I guess you're stronger than my sister. Not that it means anything. And I bet she'll whup your butt in another year."

"You little shiiiiiiiiiit!" he screeches, frantically bashing his sword in my direction.

I parry his advances before kicking him lightly in the shin—snapping my leg forward quickly as though on reflex.

"Gwah, ah! Why...?" the Boss whimpers, curling into a fetal position and clutching his leg.

Blood drips from his shin and pools on the ground.

It's a cheap trick, you know. I have a blade as sharp as an ice pick sticking out from my toes.

The second handy-dandy feature of the slime sword is that I can wield my blade from wherever and whenever I want. I thought this tactic showed the most potential. All I have to do is get in front of the enemy and slash him with the sword in my shoe, since lower-body attacks are hard to block. I parry hits, lock blades, and give my opponent a kick. It's nothing flashy, but it gets the job done.

"I guess we're through."

"W-wait...!"

"You didn't even last two minutes," I note before kicking the Boss in the chin with the blade on my foot.

Death by impalement.

He twitches as I roll him to the side and rummage through his loot.

"Artwork? I can't sell that. Hard pass on food. Come on. Where are the cash, jewels, and precious metals? Gimme, gimme, gimme."

There are several carriages' worth of spoils. And many dead merchants.

I whisper to the corpses, "I've avenged you. Now you can rest, knowing your treasures will be put to good use. I hope you make it to heaven."

I gather my haul and pray in silence. I'm guessing I found about five million *zeni*. One *zeni* is more or less equal to one Japanese yen. All this will help fund my activities as a shadowbroker. You know, the world would be a much better place if it were overrun by criminals. Oh, how I wish life were like a video game and I could encounter enemies by walking down the street.

"Please wreak more havoc in your next life," I say to the Boss, giving him a thumbs-up, when I notice...something past my fingertip.

"Is that...a cage?"

It looks sturdy and pretty big.

"Did they have slaves? Eh, hard pass on anything I can't trade for cash."

But what if there's something valuable inside? I lift its cover.

"Well, this is...unexpected."

I'm not sure how to describe it, but this cage holds...a mound of rotting flesh. I can kinda tell it's human maybe, but no clue as to its age or gender.

But it's alive. Wait, it might even be conscious. I peer into the cage, and the flesh jolts all of a sudden.

I've heard of the Church executing these creatures. I think they're called the "possessed." They're born as normal humans until their flesh rots out of nowhere, fated for death. But the Church goes out of its way to purchase them, executing them in the name of purification. They claim they're exorcising demons, but they're really just murdering the sick. But the ignorant masses applaud and praise them for keeping peace on earth. It's just as you'd expect from the Middle Ages. What a friggin' downer.

I bet I'd get more *zeni* than this entire load of spoils if I were to sell this to the Church, but that's pointless to say since I can't sell it.

Well, I guess I should put it out of its misery.

I stick my slime sword into the cage…when I notice something else.

Namely, this mound of flesh contains an abundance of magic. I've been training my magic since childhood, but this surpasses mine—it's honestly beastly. And this…

"Is this wavelength…the effects of a magical overload?"

I guess a magical overload must be the reason this turned into a pile of flesh. I've suffered its effects firsthand before. If I hadn't gotten it under control back then, I might've ended up suffering the same fate.

I know magic has certain effects on the body, which I felt all too well that fated day. I could sense its potential to raise my tolerance for magic and allow me to handle more of it, but it would be too dangerous to induce a magical overload. I'd tossed the idea.

But if I were to hypothetically conduct experiments on a product of this phenomenon…I can get closer to being a shadow commander without any risks.

"I can use this…," I say as I reach out to the flesh and infuse it with magic.

Wow, it's been a whole month, huh…? I think as I recall my first encounter with the mound and heave a sigh, back in the same abandoned village.

I wonder why things turned out this way.

All my experiments on the flesh were going swimmingly—well, until recently. I spent my days pumping the flesh with magical energy. I mean, it wasn't *my* body, so I could go buck wild on it. I was plugging away at my little experiment, testing this and that. In all honesty, it was fun. After all, one of my greatest joys in life is sensing that I'm getting closer to the essence of magic and watching my power grow before my eyes. I pushed forward, inching toward the boundaries of magic with more precision, power, and detail, until I finally had the magical overload under the tip of my thumb when…a blond elven girl appeared.

I guess it would be more accurate to say I was too fixated on improving my command of magic to notice the flesh was a blond elf until that moment. Huh. To think that stinking pile of flesh would return to its original form. I tried sending her off with a lighthearted farewell—you know, the typical *You're a free elf* and *Happy trails* and *You've got a bright future ahead of you.* But she said she didn't have a home, insisting on repaying me for saving her life, which, er, I didn't actually do. It was all a coincidence.

I considered ditching her before things got annoying, but I ended up making her Shadowbroker Subordinate A. I mean, she doesn't strike me as the type to betray me, and she seems smart… There's something about her that makes me suspect she has *too* much talent.

And even though she's also ten years old, she's more than enough proof that elves develop faster mentally than humans.

"And from this day forward, you will be Alpha."

A or Alpha. Either works.

"Understood," she replies with a nod.

She's your stereotypical elf—a beauty with blond hair, blue eyes, and fair skin.

"And your job is…" I stop to think for a moment.

This is a big one. Her job is to be the assistant to a shadow commander. No mistakes there. Which means I gotta set the scene by answering some basic questions. Like, what exactly is an eminence in shadow? And what purpose do they serve?

Flushing out the appropriate narrative is key. I mean, if I said I was fighting to get revenge for losing at pachinko slots, I wouldn't seem too cool, right?

I have to choose wisely. I mean, all my daydreams are filled with puppeteers from even before I came into this world and certainly after. I've

mixed and matched thousands—no, tens of thousands—of possible scenarios in my mind. And I have the perfect one for the occasion.

"To hide in the shadows and prevent the resurrection of Diablos the demon."

"Diablos the demon...?" Alpha cocks her head in confusion.

"I'm sure you've heard of him. You know, the stories of long, long ago. Diablos brought our world to the brink of destruction when three brave warriors—a human, an elf, and a therianthrope, or a hybrid beast—teamed up to destroy him and protected the world."

"Oh yeah. But isn't that a fairy tale?"

"Nope, it really happened. But the truth is way more complicated than that...," I continue, as a small, wry smile appears on my face. I mean, getting to my level and twisting out a scenario from a legend is a piece of cake.

"Just before the heroes slayed the demon, with his very last breath, he put a curse on them, which is known as the Curse of Diablos."

"The Curse of Diablos? I've never heard of that before."

"Oh, but it exists. It's the curse of the possessed...and the very disease that ravished your body."

"What? No way..." Alpha goes bug-eyed in horror.

"The descendants of the heroes have suffered from this illness. Back in the day, the Curse of Diablos used to be curable. Just like yours."

No one would believe that Alpha was possessed until recently. Her smooth and unblemished skin is evidence to back up my story.

I mean, even though this is a big fat lie.

"It's proof that one is a descendant of the heroes who saved the world. You know, the possessed used to be lauded, appreciated, and protected—in the past."

"But no one appreciates us anymore, let alone..." Alpha trails off, screwing up her face.

"There's someone out there who twisted history—erasing the truth about the lineage of the possessed and hiding the cure to the curse. What's worse, these people became targets of shame."

"Ngh...! Who would do such a thing?!"

"Those who scheme to resurrect Diablos. That's because those with the curse carry the bloodline of the heroes and high levels of magical energy. In other words, they serve as a major military force for us. On the flip side, they're a nuisance to his supporters."

"Which is why we're called the possessed and disposed of…"

"Exactly. You lost your hometown and family—all because you've been accused of committing a false sin. Aren't they despicable?"

"Yeah. There's no way I wouldn't find them absolutely detestable."

"The Cult of Diablos. That's our enemy. They only work behind the scenes, which is why we must conceal ourselves, too. Lurk in the darkness and hunt down shadows."

"I'm guessing they've gotta be formidable if they have enough say to pull the strings behind the scenes. Which means that our enemies hold positions of power…and that hordes of people under their control don't know the truth…"

I nod seriously. "Our journey may be perilous. But we must go forward. Are you with me?"

"If that's what you want, then I'll devote my life to it. We'll punish these sinners with death…" Alpha stares at me with her intense blue eyes and smiles defiantly. Her face is lovely even in its youth and teems with determination and resolve.

I fist pump in my mind. *Whoo-hoo! This elf girl is super-gullible!*

Obviously, the Cult of Diablos doesn't exist, which means we'll never find them. It also provides grounds for me to accuse and slaughter any thief syndicate in the area for being in the Cult. And I bet we can stake out battles between fighters and intervene as shadow commanders. And—and we can say fake-deep stuff for our parting words! Like *The end is near…* Or *The resurrection of the demon is nigh…* And it would be so cool if we could arrive with the wind on a battlefield, saying *You fools… You're being controlled…*, before completely wiping everyone out…! Wow. I could honestly go on and on.

Right. I almost forgot. The most important part. This name of this organization…

"We are the Shadow Garden… We lurk in the darkness and hunt down shadows…"

"The Shadow Garden. That's a nice name."

I know, right? It's sick.

This is the very moment the Shadow Garden and the World's Greatest Enemy—the Cult of Diablos—is born. I move one step closer to becoming a mastermind.

"I guess we can start by wielding our magic and practicing sparring with each other. I'll act as the main fighter in battle, but you've got to get stronger to wrangle in the small fry."

"I know. We've got a tough enemy on our hands. I have to raise the bar for myself."

"Right. That's the spirit."

"And we have to find other descendants of heroes and protect them."

"Uh, erm, yeah. All in moderation."

It would be fun to play shadowbroker with more people, since that'd make it feel more like a legit organization. But I don't need that many people. I honestly wouldn't have a problem if it just stayed the two of us.

"Well, for now, let's just focus on getting stronger," I suggest, readying my wooden sword.

I block Alpha's attack, which has an unexpected bite to it. To think she was only a novice until recently. Alpha has a good feel for things and plenty of magical energy, which means I can make good use of her.

Under the moonlight, I swing my wooden sword as these thoughts run through my mind.

The Eminence in Shadow

nestly can't remember what catalyzed this desire.

l know is I've admired shadowbrokers for as long as

n remember.

s it a certain anime? Or was it a manga—or a movie?

I guess it doesn't matter. I was all in for anything that featured a

stermind, or an eminence in shadow, as I like to call them. These

racters were never the protagonists or final bosses but were relegated to a role

ind the scenes where they flaunted their powers and meddled in the

irs of others. I've always looked up to the men in the shadows.

anted to be one of them.

All I know is I've admired shadowbrokers for as long as

I can remember.

Was it a certain anime? Or was it a manga—or a movie?

Eh, I guess it doesn't matter. I was all in for anything that featured a

mastermind, or an eminence in shadow, as I like to call them. These

characters were never the protagonists or final bosses but were relegated to a role

behind the scenes where they flaunted their powers and meddled in the

affairs of others. I've always looked up to the men in the shadows.

I wanted to be one of them.

Think of children who worship their favorite superheroes.

That was me but with master puppeteers.

Starting the Shadowbroker Tutorial!

Chapter 1

The Eminence in Shadow

Chapter 1

It's been three years since the establishment of the Shadow Garden—give or take. Alpha and I turned thirteen years old, and my older sister Claire, fifteen.

There isn't anything special about turning thirteen, but fifteen is another story. That's when aristocrats begin their three-year education at a school in the royal capital. As the bearer of the hopes and dreams of the Kagenou household, Claire had a crazy farewell party thrown for her, which was organized by our mother. Like, wow, you can't get more clichéd than that.

And that's fine. Well, it was fine until she vanished the day of her departure. Read: All hell broke loose in the Kagenou household.

"The room was like this when I came in," explains my dad in a low, suave voice. His face isn't bad, either. "No signs of a struggle. But it looks like the window has been pried open. The culprit must have been skilled to do this without me and Claire noticing."

He touches the windowsill and stares wistfully at the sky. A glass of whiskey would complete the scene.

Now, if only he had hair…

"And?" replies a chilly voice. "Are you saying we're out of luck since the kidnapper was skilled?"

That was my mom.

"Th-that's not what I'm saying. I was just stating a fact…," answers my dad as cold sweat drips down his cheeks.

There's a pause.

"Shut it, baldyyyyyy!!"

"Eep! I-I'm sorry! I'm sorry!!"

By the way, it's like I'm invisible. They don't expect much from me, and I don't cause any trouble. I'm trying to keep this up to lie low in the background.

It's really too bad that my sister disappeared, since she was cool and all. But they nabbed her in the middle of the night when I was out training in the abandoned town, which meant I couldn't do anything to stop it. After watching with a concerned expression while my parents bicker, I sneak into my room and roll into bed.

"You can come out now."

"Okay," replies a voice accompanied by the sound of the curtains swishing gently.

A girl in a black slime bodysuit steps out from behind them.

"Oh, it's you. Beta."

"Yes," says a girl, an elf like Alpha.

But while Alpha's hair is blond, Beta's is silver, framing her blue feline eyes and the mole right under one of them. She's the third member of the Shadow Garden, after me and Alpha. I know I told Alpha to do things in moderation, but I swear, she keeps taking people in like they're stray cats or something.

"Where's Alpha?"

"She's searching for signs of Miss Claire."

"Dang, she's fast. Is my sister alive?"

"Most likely."

"Can we rescue her?"

"It's possible...but it requires your assistance, Master Shadow."

Oh, I have them call me Shadow. It's fitting for the leader of the Shadow Garden, right?

"Did Alpha say that?"

"Yes. She said we must take every precaution in a hostage situation."

"Huh."

If I'm being honest, Alpha is plenty powerful on her own. If she's asking for backup, we must be dealing with a big shot.

"It makes my blood boil...," I say, compressing the magic in my hand down further. In a flash, I release it, causing the air to quiver around us.

There's no particular reason for that. I just love to put on a good show.

Plus, it startles Beta, who even murmurs, "Incredible." Nice.

As of late, I haven't run out of training partners with Alpha, Beta, and Delta around, but I do like switching things up every once in a while. And I'm obsessed with playing the part of a mastermind, which makes this a perfect opportunity.

"It's been a while since I've showed my true strength...," I mumble.

At this point, I'm used to giving off a mysterious vibe. And with Alpha and Beta creating an optimal environment for pretend play, I've been very hyped up lately.

"As we'd expected, the perpetrator is a member of the Cult of Diablos—presumably one of their highest-ranking officers."

"A high rank, huh...? But what do they want with my sister?"

"They must suspect that she's one of the heroes' descendants."

"Well, those bastards guessed right..."

And that's how she thickens the plot.

On top of that, she takes out a pile of documents and starts saying all kinds of cryptic things.

Like "Your story was true after all..."

And "The Children of Diablos from one thousand years ago have..."

And "This monument may be a sign of the Cult...," but I don't know for sure, 'cause I can't read ancient texts. I have a feeling that Alpha can't even understand them.

Y'know, I bet the two of them scrounged up some paperwork that looked appropriately suspicious to feel as if we're getting closer to the truth. Yeah, that sounds about right.

"Take a look at this report. According to our most recent investigation, Miss Claire seems to have been brought to this hideout..."

Beta begins laying out a huge heap of files. It's complete gibberish to me. The majority is written in an ancient alphabet, and the others are a series of nonsensical numbers and symbols. Dang, they really have a knack for creating fake reports. In this regard, they're way better than me.

I ignore her explanation and chuck a small knife at the map on my wall. I aim for wherever feels right or something.

Zing. It sinks into the map.

"There."

"There? What are you…?"

"That's where my sister is."

"But there's nothing… Wait. No way…!" She balks, hastily rummaging through her reports as if she's realized something.

Erm, ah, it's really just a random throw. But Beta is a great actress.

Lemme take a guess. You're gonna say the secret hideout is located right at the tip of the knife, right?

"After cross-referencing my reports, it appears the hideout is at that location."

See? What did I say?

"To think you instantly interpreted these documents and uncovered hidden details… You never cease to amaze me."

"Beta, you gotta train more."

"I'll do my best."

Bravo! I know it's all an act, but whew! It pulls on my heartstrings. Oh, Beta! You've got me on the edge of my seat.

"I'll report to Alpha right away. Will we attempt our rescue tonight?"

"Yeah."

Beta bows to me and leaves the room with eyes all sparkly. Like, I can almost feel that you totally respect me.

Cheers to her Academy Award–winning performance!

A man walks down a dimly lit underground tunnel. Appearing to be in his late thirties, he has a piercing gaze and a well-built body, and all his gray hair is slicked back.

He stops at the end of the tunnel, where there's one door flanked by two soldiers.

"The daughter of Baron Kagenou," he orders.

"In here, sir," one soldier pipes up, bowing to Grease and unlocking the door. "We've got her restrained, but she's extremely hostile. Please proceed with caution."

"Hmph. Who do you think I am?"

"M-my apologies, sir!"

Grease pushes through the door and enters the stone dungeon, where a girl is shackled to the wall with magic chains.

"You must be Claire Kagenou."

When she's addressed by her name, the girl looks up at Grease in response.

She's stunning, wrapped in the dainty negligee she wore to bed. It lightly veils her voluptuous breasts and shapely thighs, and her silken black hair is cut straight across her back.

Claire glares defiantly at him. "I've seen you around the capital. You're Viscount Grease, aren't you?"

"Oh, well, I used to be a royal guard…or you saw me at the Bushin Festival."

"Right, the tournament. Princess Iris really tore you a new one." Claire smirks.

"Hmph. We're bound by tournament rules, which makes that an exception. I would never lose to her in a real battle."

"You would lose then, too, Viscount Grease…you first-round flunker."

"Shut it. A brat will never know the struggles of getting to the finals." Grease scowls at Claire.

"I'll make it in a year."

"I hate to break it to you, but you don't have a year left."

The chains that bind her clang loudly as she closes the distance between them, snapping her teeth a hairbreadth away from the nape of Grease's neck.

Chomp.

If Grease hadn't slightly turned his head, she would have severed his carotid artery.

"Which of us won't see another year? Want to test it out?"

"You won't be testing anything out, Claire Kagenou."

Claire is howling with laughter when he punches her in the jaw, slamming her against the stone wall. But her glare remains unchanged and locked on Grease the entire time.

His next punch doesn't land.

"Jumping backward now, eh?"

Claire smiles fearlessly. "Oh, I assumed you were trying to hit a fly."

"Hmph. I guess you're not letting your strong magical powers overwhelm you."

"I learned that it's all about how you use magic, not how much."

"Your father taught you well."

"Baldy didn't teach me a thing. I'm talking about my brother."

"Your brother...?"

"He's a cheeky one. I win every time we battle, but I'm the one learning from his techniques, not the other way around. Which is why I make life hard for him." A playful grin splays across her face.

"My condolences to your brother. I guess this makes me the hero who saves him from his wicked sister. Enough chitchat..." Grease pauses, observing her intently.

"Claire Kagenou, has your physical condition...felt off recently? As in, has it gotten harder to use and handle magic? Have you experienced any pain when you use it? Is your body starting to turn dark with rot? ... Do you have any of these symptoms?"

"Did you abduct me to play doctor?" The corners of Claire's glossy lips lift to a smile.

"You know, I used to have a daughter. I don't want to knock you around more than I already have. Answering honestly would benefit us both."

"Is that a threat? When I feel threatened, I tend to get hostile...even when I shouldn't."

"Are you saying you won't tell me the truth?"

"We'll see."

Grease and Claire glare at each other for a while.

She's the one to break the silence. "Fine. I'll answer your dumb question, since it's no big deal. What was it? About my condition and magic, right? Well, everything's fine now. If I wasn't chained up, I'd be doing pretty darn good."

"What do you mean by 'now'?"

"Well, I first noticed the symptoms a year ago."

"What? Are you saying it got cured—on its own?" Grease has never heard of a case where *it* healed on its own.

"Yeah, I didn't do anything to… Oh, right. What was it? A 'stretch'? I don't know what that means, but my little bro asked me to stretch with him, and I felt better after that."

"Stretch? I've never heard of that before…but if you had symptoms, that means I wasn't mistaken in thinking you're compatible."

"Compatible…? What does that mean?"

"Nothing that should concern you. Either way, you're going to break soon enough. Oh, and I'll make sure to look into your brother…"

Before he can finish his sentence, he suffers a blow to the nose.

"Wha—?!" he barks, stumbling back to the door and glowering at Claire. He holds his bloody nose. "Claire Kagenou, you wretch…!"

All four limbs should have been bound, but she somehow managed to free her right arm, where blood trickles down her wrist.

"You scraped off your own flesh and dislocated your finger…?!"

These are no ordinary chains. They're sealed with magic. In other words, she unleashed the full extent of her physical strength to slice the flesh off her hand, break her own bones, and slide out of the chains to punch Grease. This rattles him to his core.

"If you do anything to my brother, I'll never forgive you! I'll kill you, your loved ones, your family, your friends… Ngh…?!"

Grease clobbers Claire in the gut with all his might. There's no way she can defend herself from his spells, especially when she's strapped down by chains.

"You bitch…!" spits Grease as she crumples to the ground.

On the floor, there's a pool of dark-red blood fed by a trickle from her right hand.

"Well, then. I'll know when I've used this...," he murmurs, reaching out to touch her blood when a winded soldier flings the door open.

"Viscount Grease, we're in trouble! Intruders!"

"Intruders?! Who the hell are they?"

"We don't know! There are only a few of them, but we don't stand a chance without you!"

"Ugh, I'll take care of it! The rest of you, stay on guard!" Grease clicks his tongue in irritation before turning on his heel and making his way from the cell.

By the time Grease arrives on the scene, the area is already smeared with blood.

The soldiers who protect the major facility aren't weak by any means, and some even rival the royal guard.

"Why? This can't be...!"

Illuminated by a single light streaming in from the outside, countless dead bodies litter the ground of the underground hall in the facility.

Each bears a single slash—sliced by an unimaginably destructive force.

"Son of a bitch...!"

Grease glares at a group of figures dressed in black bodysuits. From their curves, he can guess they're petite girls—seven in total. Under the dim light of the moon, they're stealthy enough that it's easy to lose sight of them without a concerted effort. These women are using a rare technique to control their magical presence, and Grease recognizes this group might just rival him in strength.

There's one who's drenched in blood, eyeing him under the moonlight.

"Nnr...!"

In this moment, instinct overtakes Grease—not for any explicit reason, but he can sense danger.

Blood drips down her bodysuit and onto the floor, and she lets her katana drag behind her apathetically, creating a trail of gore.

"Who the hell are you? What's your purpose?" he asks, attempting to suppress his unease.

But he's faced with seven rivals as powerful as him. To fight would be asinine. Grease curses his bad luck as he searches for a way out.

The blood-splattered girl isn't listening to him. She laughs, snickering from behind her bloodied mask.

She's going to hunt me down...! Grease thinks, just as he hears another voice.

"Back off, Delta."

The girl halts in place before retreating without resistance. Grease lets out a huge sigh of relief.

Another girl walks forward to take her place.

"We are the Shadow Garden."

If they were anywhere else, her angelic voice would have entranced him.

"I'm Alpha."

He realizes she's revealed her face at some point, and her pale skin gleams under the moonlight. She steps forward.

"Nn...!"

He sees she's an elf with golden hair and beauty that leaves him gasping for breath.

She takes another step.

"Our purpose...is to eliminate the Cult of Diablos."

He doesn't take notice of her black sword until it slices through the air and parts the night sky. Or at least, it seems to create that illusion, and Grease is overcome with intimidation by the force of her swing and the wind that follows it.

How did she acquire such power at this age? He trembles with jealousy and fear—but more than anything, he's petrified by her declaration.

"How...how do you know our group?"

The Cult of Diablos. Grease is one of the few people in the facility who knows the name of this organization.

"We know everything. We know all about Diablos the demon, his curse, and the heroes' descendants. And…the truth about the possessed."

"H-how did you…?"

Grease was only recently informed of this top secret information, which couldn't— No, *shouldn't* have been leaked.

"You're not the only ones after the Curse of Diablos."

"Ksh…!"

He knows he can't forgive them for getting access to classified information. But would slaying them prevent it from spreading?

No, no good.

Which means he needs to live—to survive to inform headquarters about the girls, which is why Grease moves forward.

"Aaaaaaaaagh!!" he shouts, unsheathing his sword and swiping at Alpha.

"How reckless," she notes, dodging and countering it with ease.

Her blade grazes his cheek, where blood pours from the fresh wound.

And yet, that doesn't stop him. He continues to pursue victory, even as none of his attacks land. Grease misses by a hairbreadth each time.

On the other side, Alpha is focused on eliminating unnecessary movements and calculating the trajectory of his sword to sidestep oncoming assaults.

And all the while, Grease's arms are slashed, legs cut, shoulders sliced.

But none of his wounds are fatal.

Grease sneers when he realizes she won't kill him until she gets intel out of him, and a new path to victory comes into view. After he slices through nothing again and again, he's finally slashed in the chest, causing him to retreat.

"Let's not waste any more time," says Alpha.

Grease doesn't answer, kneeling and clutching his wounded chest. A smile then spreads across his face…and he swallows something.

"What…are you doing?!"

His body doubles in size—his complexion darkens, his muscles bulge, his eyes glow red. And most importantly, his magic capacity increases...dramatically.

"Unnh...!"

Grease's steel sword zings through the air without warning, which Alpha manages to block instantly. But she grimaces on impact, using the momentum to leap back and create distance between them.

"Interesting trick," she notes, shaking her arm as pins and needles shoot through it. She cocks her head to the side. "Based on the wave frequency, I'm guessing it's a magical overload...that's been forcibly induced..."

"Lady Alpha, is everything all right?" asks a voice from behind, surprised to see Alpha back down during a fight for the first time.

"It's fine, Beta. Just a messy situation... Hmm?"

When Alpha turns her gaze back to Grease, there's no one in sight. Well, more accurately, there's a rectangular hole in his place, leading to a lower level of the facility—a trapdoor.

"...He got away."

"Yeah...let's go after him," Beta responds, ready to leap in behind him.

Alpha stops her in the nick of time. "That won't be necessary. He'll take care of it."

"He...? Now that I think about it, Master Shadow said he'd go ahead of us... No way."

"Yeah. I have to admit I was worried he'd get lost when he sprinted down a different route." Alpha giggles.

"He knew this would happen... He's done it again."

Their eyes glow with respect as they peer down the hole together.

"I'm lost," I mumble to myself in an empty underground facility.

It was all fine and well when we infiltrated the hideout, but I got sick of fighting off small fry. I thought I'd go ahead and kill their boss, which brings us…here. Bummer. I mean, I even practiced what I'd say when I faced their leader and everything.

Anyway, this place is huge. I get the vibe of a group of bandits living in an abandoned military facility.

"Hmm?"

I sense someone running toward me from the other side of the tunnel. It takes a few beats before the figure notices me, too, leaving a wide gap between us.

"You've been expecting me…," he assumes.

He's super-jacked, and his eyes have a crimson glow for some reason or another. He looks…really friggin' cool. I can imagine him shooting laser beams with his eyes.

"But if it's just you, this should be a breeze," he remarks with a twisted smile on his face.

Then he vanishes—well, more like moves fast enough that an average person would've thought he disappeared.

But I parry his attack with one hand. As long as I can spot the course of the attack, I'm not scared by the velocity of the assault. Even power is all about how you use it.

"Nnr!" he yelps.

I push him away in the shoulder and retreat.

His magic is incredible—much stronger than Alpha, if I'm being honest. But his command over it is dismal, unfortunately. He's nothing but a dope jacked with magic.

I'm not a big fan of people who go bananas with their magic, getting yoked with spells and moving at unimaginable speeds, and I don't like relying on physical force. Not that I'm trying to reject it. I mean, if I was forced to choose between strength and technique, I'd take strength in a heartbeat, since advanced tactics without the power to back them up are useless.

That said, I absolutely despise half-baked strategies that solely depend on physical abilities—like power alone, or speed alone, or reaction time alone. They overlook and disregard the subtleties of battle.

You see, strength is natural, but mastery requires effort. Shadowbrokers never lose when it comes to skill and expertise. And I want to be the same. My techniques will bolster my strength. My ingenuity will dictate speed. My reaction time will let me scope out potential attacks. Physicality is important, but I'd never screw up a fight by relying on it. That's all part of my battle aesthetic.

If I'm being honest, this hulky slugger is starting to piss me off.

Let's teach him a lesson…about the right way to use magic.

"Lesson one."

I wield my slime sword and walk forward—one step, two steps, three.

On that last one, he takes a swing at me, which means I'm in his fighting range and is my cue to speed up. I take the tiniest quantity of magic possible, focus it in my feet, compress, and then release it in one shot. That's all there is to it, and you can create an explosive impact with the smallest magical force.

His sword slices through the air.

And now he's in my range.

I don't need speed or power or magic. I graze his neck with my ebony katana, slicing through the topmost layer of skin and leaving the veins untouched.

I back up. His blade scathes my cheek at the same time.

"Lesson two."

I make my move as he readies his sword again. I don't use magic, letting his movements stay quicker than mine. But he can't attack and move at the same time—no matter his speed.

Which is why I can get closer and take one tiny step.

It's a distance that's too long for me and too short for him.

There's a moment of silence that follows.

I see him looking uncertain of his next move, but he ultimately chooses to back away.

I knew he was going to do that, based on the shift of magical energy inside him, and I close the distance before he has a chance to back up.

This time, my sword scrapes against his leg, cutting a little deeper than the last laceration.

"Gah…!" He groans in pain and continues his retreat.

I don't pursue him.

"Lesson three."

I'm just getting started.

Have I ever felt this overpowered before? Grease wonders as the ink-black sword continues to break skin.

Even when he fought Alpha the elf, even when the princess claimed victory at the Bushin Festival, Grease didn't feel weak. In fact, the last time he'd felt a power imbalance…was when he was a kid. It was the first time he'd ever held a sword and squared off with his mentor—an adult versus a child, a champion versus a novice. It was hardly anything that could be considered a fight.

Grease is experiencing that same feeling right about now.

The boy in front of him doesn't look tough whatsoever. At the very least, he doesn't emit the same menacing aura as Alpha when Grease fought her. He's a total natural; his stance, magic, and swordsmanship all seem to come effortlessly. In fact, his strength and speed are unremarkable, honestly—nothing special at all. But his strategy perfects his swordplay. And he manages to stand against Grease's powers of mass destruction using that alone.

Which makes Grease feel an overwhelming sense of defeat.

He knows the only reason he's alive is because the boy allows it. If his opponent wanted it, Grease would be dead in an instant.

But Grease could regenerate his body as long as he didn't suffer fatal wounds. Of course, there are limits and nasty side effects. Meanwhile, he's shed pails of blood and had his bones broken, his flesh shredded, which means he'll need more time to fully recover.

But even in this time of crisis, Grease survives.

No. It's more accurate to say he's been spared.

*   *   *

Grease lets out a single question: "Why…?"

Why are you letting me live?

Why are we enemies?

Why are you so strong?

Why?

The young boy shrouded in black looks down at Grease. "Lurk in the darkness and hunt down shadows. That's the only reason we exist."

There's a distant sadness to his voice.

And that's all it takes for Grease to understand the situation.

"Are you going up against them…?" he asks.

There are certain people in this world who the law cannot touch. Grease knew this and considered himself above that threshold—special concessions, privileges, and those with hidden personas. After all, the light of the law doesn't shine to the very edge of the world.

While Grease enjoyed certain privileges, he was trampled and crushed by those at the top, which made him yearn for more power…and led to his downfall.

"Even if you… Even if your gang of twats becomes stronger, you'll never defeat them. The darkness of this world…is a deeper abyss than your wildest dreams," he says—not to warn the boy but to express his diabolical hopes.

Grease wants the boy to get pulverized, lose everything, and become totally disillusioned with society. But, overcome with petty envy and spite, he frets that this wish is out of reach.

"Then we dive deeper," offers the boy without a hint of eagerness or ambitiousness.

But Grease can sense his steadfast resolve and unshakable confidence.

"It's not easy."

Unacceptable.

Utterly unacceptable, thinks Grease, who's doomed for attempting to take them down himself.

This is the moment he decides to cross the final frontier. He removes a pill from his breast pocket and swallows it whole when he realizes he's not going to survive. *If that's the case*, he thinks, *I'll use this life to teach him the truth.*

The truth about the darkness of this world.

The aura surrounding Grease changes.

Until now, his magical energy had been rampaging around his body, but it starts to withdraw, replaced by its densely compressed twin. His veins rupture and burst with blood, his muscles tear, his bones shatter—but his body heals instantly. He defies the physical limitations of a human form and hosts an immeasurable amount of magical power.

The Cult calls this the "awakening."

Once one assumes this form, there's no turning back. But in return... one is bestowed with Herculean strength.

"Aaaaghhh!" Grease roars in a beastly fashion before vanishing into thin air.

The dull sound of impact hangs in the air. In the same moment, the boy in black is flung off his feet toward a wall, which he kicks to shift his body and land on the ground.

But Grease continues swinging at him, propelling the boy back again.

"Too slow! Too flimsy! Too frail! This is reality!" Grease aggressively hounds him.

With another *thump*, the boy is catapulted backward by more of Grease's attacks—quick, heavy, and merciless. It's all because he possesses an overwhelming force.

Grease thinks he has it all figured out: The tiger doesn't have to be cunning to kill a hare. He just needs strength. By pushing back, it makes it impossible for the boy to fight—and he's destined to fall apart.

But this is all wrong.

"Hgh?!" Grease whines as blood erupts from his chest.

He takes notice of a laceration—one that breaks past the surface of his skin. Grease halts in place for a split second, but he recovers fast enough to knock his enemy back in the next instant.

"It's hopeless! You can't get me!!" he shrieks, even as his flesh is shredded down to his bones.

But his wounds begin to bubble up and heal in the next beat.

"This is true power! This is true strength!!" Grease starts to accelerate, slashing his weapon through the air, even as blood spouts from his body.

He appears as a flash of scarlet light.

Ebony and crimson—the two colors clash, causing the one in black to get slung back and the one in red to spew fresh blood.

Their battle is too quick for the human eye to catch, and the afterimage of crimson and the backward movements of ebony are the only indicators of something uncanny in the making.

Their skirmish doesn't last long. There's a clear power imbalance, and it's easy to guess that the figure in black would be the one to break. It's a fight that the one in red shouldn't have lost—slinging his sword on repeat and pulverizing the other into submission with his cataclysmic strength.

But why?

Why does he look unfazed…?

"Why…why can't I hit you…?"

The boy in black hasn't changed from the beginning of the fight. He's barely unleashed any magic or moved on his own accord, instead choosing to go with the flow and let Grease fling him around. It's as if he's a fallen leaf swept away in a rapid stream.

Except he's not completely passive. He uses the momentum of these blows to land a direct hit—without seeming showy or expending any unnecessary energy.

It's natural. As if it's supposed to happen.

"Terrible," states the boy in black, staring down Grease and looking as if he can read his thoughts.

"You know nothing… Nothing, you bastard!" Grease barks back, pooling every bit of magic into his body and sword before taking his shot.

He's ready to eliminate this boy, even if it costs him his life, raring for the biggest assault of his existence.

"No more games."

Grease is sliced in two—by an unconstrained swing of a sword. It's hurled down on him with the ease of a walk in the park. A singular stroke bisects it all—his sword, his enhanced magical powers, his muscular physique.

The viscount thought the reason behind the boy's advanced swordplay was pure skill—not magic, strength, or speed. But he's wrong.

"What is this…?"

It's a single stroke that destroys everything.

Grease watches the blade cut through his sword, his magic, his flesh, and his bones as he stands on the verge of death. It's a strike fortified with impenetrable magic, titanic strength, sonic speed, and most importantly…natural talent.

It's perfect.

The boy in black has everything at his disposal. But he chose not to use all of it until now.

Nothing could withstand that single stroke containing every ounce of his power.

"I guess…this is it…," mutters Grease as blood rushes out of him, and his upper body topples and hits the ground. There's a beat before his other half crashes to the floor.

Grease tries to regenerate the bisection, but nothing is salvageable. His flesh is putrid and rotten, excreting black fluid that soaks the area around him.

Ebony looks down. Grease glances up.

Having crossed swords with the boy in black, the viscount understands that one's temperament can be seen through one's swordplay. His

opponent appears as a serious, naive nobody—who trained with blood, sweat, and tears to reign victorious in battle.

I thought he was just a brat who knew nothing, but I was wrong.

His enemy had known everything and had still chosen to fight.

Powerless, he thinks of himself. He's been powerless for his entire life. He's tried to succeed but returned empty-handed, while this whelp in black…

"Mi…llia…" Grease groans, reaching for a dagger encrusted with a blue jewel and closing his eyes.

As consciousness slips away from him, he sees the smiling face of his beloved daughter who passed long ago.

Anyway, that's how we ended our slaughter of some bandits—I mean, our little rescue mission.

I found my sister totally unconscious, so I undid her chains and left her there, which contributed to her crankiness when she returned home the next day. But she's a real tough cookie—tough enough that the wound on her hand almost healed overnight.

After a hectic week or so of hospital treatments and follow-up investigations, my sister finally made her way to the capital—though she pestered me more than usual during that time for some annoying reason.

The girls in the Shadow Garden were busy, conducting their own research, taking care of the remaining bandits, and other stuff. Oh, right, we're not calling them bandits. Whatever. The Cult. I mean, they're all thieves in the end.

But that geezer with red eyes was outstanding. I mean, he inspired me to come up with "then we dive deeper," which sounds like something a shadowbroker would say. I owe him my thanks. I would've loved to have him play a supporting role to my part as an eminence in shadow.

This was a must-see performance. My ability to improvise and portray a master puppeteer was off the rockers. It's a real shame there wasn't a live audience. But I only have to wait two more years—which is when I go to the capital. You know the one. It's a world-famous metropolis and the only city in this country that houses one million people.

I bet protagonists are a dime a dozen, and there might be Final Bosses, too.

There's bound to be conspiracies, rebellions, and incidents—none of which would ever happen in the boonies. And that's when the mastermind bursts onto the scene… Huh. Now that I think about it, I guess I'm just a toad who feels cocky about beating some bandits. At this moment in time, my prologue hasn't even been written.

And then one day, Alpha and the other girls gather before me, just as I'm yearning to get stronger for school, which is two years down the line. They want to share their reports on the Cult and lab findings on the curse and all that jazz.

It's unusual to have all seven of them in a room at once, especially since it seems they've got their hands full as of late.

Geez, go easy on the research and investigations. I mean, it's all pointless anyway, I think as I listen to their reports.

Here's a simple summary of their findings.

Their first claim is that the heroes who slayed Diablos the demon were all women, which is why they're the ones who suffer exclusively from the curse.

How creative. But I hate to break it to you that all the heroes were men in the most common theory. Oh, wait, I bet they came up with that since the Shadow Garden is comprised of seven women apart from me.

Their next report was on how the curse was most common among elves, followed by hybrid beasts and then humans. According to their research, it has to do with the life spans of the respective species. With humans living short lives with weak traces of the heroic bloodline, they're least susceptible to the curse. On the other hand, elves have long life expectancies with potent concentrations of blood, which makes them the most prone to fall victim to the curse. The therianthropes, or hybrid beasts, are in the middle.

Now that I think about it, I'm the only human in the Shadow Garden, and I've never been possessed. Besides me, we have two therianthropes and a posse of five elves—and all seven have been possessed. You know, they did a stellar job coming up with this backstory.

And then they proceed to report on a bunch of other things, which I pretend to absorb.

They move on to their reports about the Cult, which is supposedly a massive organization that operates on a global scale. Fascinating.

In terms of being the possessed or cursed or whatever, they tell me the Cult calls them "compatibles," and their members are supposedly going the extra mile to locate, acquire, and wipe them from existence or some crap.

Anyway, they suggest that the Shadow Garden scatter across the world to prevent this from spreading. Their plan would leave me with one rotating subordinate, the rest of them scattering to every corner of the world to protect the possessed, investigate the Cult, and sabotage their activities.

When they suggest this new plan, it hits me all of a sudden: They must have realized that the Cult doesn't exist.

They're through with this stupid charade and demanding their freedom. What else could scattering across the world mean? I'm guessing they feel indebted to me for curing them, which is why they're going to stick with me on a rotating basis. I just have to deal with it. I know that's what they're trying to tell me.

I'm bummed out. In my past life, the kids idolized the heroes as much as I adored masterminds—until we grew up, and they didn't even notice that they'd forgotten all about their precious heroes. I was left alone. I guess the girls have grown up, too.

I'm feeling all soppy but agree to send them on their way. I never planned on having seven members to begin with. If they leave me with one subordinate, that's enough for me. I see them off, and we reluctantly exchange good-byes.

I make a vow to myself: I'll never stop trying to become a mastermind, even if that means I have to face this world alone.

She no longer fears killing others.

Beta whips her inky katana, splattering congealed blood off her blade and onto the ashen ground in a clean line. She stands cloaked in the darkness of night and surrounded by a group of soldiers lying facedown.

"End him," orders Beta.

The girls in black bodysuits pierce their blades into the guard. One of their hands in particular shakes violently, but it doesn't stop the girl from thrusting her sword into his pressure point.

"Guh… Gaaaah!" shrieks the soldier with his final breath, causing her blade to freeze in place.

It's the type of cry that'll haunt her in her sleep until she becomes accustomed to killing.

Beta envelops the girl's hands on the helm with her own before giving the blade a sharp twist. Together, they feel the soldier's life leaving his body.

"Ah, ahhh…!" gasps a voice.

This time, the cries are the girl's.

Beta wraps her arm around her subordinate's trembling shoulders and issues her next instructions. "Secure the target."

The group makes its way to the carriage, boarding the loading deck. Following the shrill sounds of a chain snapping, the girls emerge from the wagon with a dark mound of rotting flesh.

It's still breathing.

"Return to Lady Alpha—fast."

They haul the mound, carrying it tenderly, and start to pick up speed, followed by the member of their order previously nestled in Beta's bosom.

Beta squints slightly, watching them go.

She's raising them well.

These girls used to know nothing about combat. They'd never held a sword, and it goes without saying that they'd never murdered anyone before meeting her.

Beta is reminded of her own past, and old memories begin to resurface.

She still remembers how it felt when she killed for the first time—her sword piercing their heart, their hand grabbing hers. Beta couldn't believe the strength of their grip even as they suffered a fatal wound.

"There's a short period of time when people can move after they've been stabbed through the heart. Don't let your guard down. Hey, Beta, are you listening?"

Beta was listening to Alpha's calm voice but couldn't understand what she meant for the life of her.

She was paralyzed with fear—incapable of moving or thinking.

"You're impossible."

The head of her enemy soared through the air.

Alpha had beheaded him.

The corpse dropped to the floor, spurting blood that splatted Beta, and large teardrops fell from her eyes.

"Find a reason to fight."

Those words sounded so cold.

Beta was a child who had trouble doing things on her own.

After joining the Shadow Garden, she always followed Alpha around. After all, they were old acquaintances, and she knew she would go down the right path if she stuck by Alpha's side.

But Beta couldn't find a reason to fight by following Alpha's footsteps—or understand the importance of finding said motivation. As a result, she couldn't get used to the idea of murder, vomiting violently after killing someone on a mission and shaking in fear every night as she tried to fall asleep. It wasn't unusual for her to wake up screaming in the middle of the night.

On one particular evening, Shadow approached the tormented girl.

"Do you seek wisdom...?"

"Y-yes?" Beta answered all jittery as she cocked her head to the side.

In her eyes, he was enigmatic and extremely powerful.

"If you seek wisdom...I shall give it to you."

He might mean the knowledge of easing my emotional turmoil from murdering others, she thought.

With great expectations, Beta nodded. "I—I want wisdom." Her voice trembled.

"Then I shall give it to you..."

Shadow began telling a story. "Once upon a time, in a faraway place, there was an old man and an old woman..."

It was an ordinary fairy tale—no smidgen of wisdom or anything else.

What the heck?

She wasn't sure how to respond—not that she was brave enough to oppose the one revered by Alpha—and shut her trap to listen to his story. It was more interesting than she'd initially imagined. In fact, she realized she'd been so absorbed in the tale that she'd forgotten the time.

That evening, Beta had a deep, peaceful night's rest.

And ever since then, Shadow recited a bedside story to Beta before she went to sleep.

Beta had always been a bookworm, but she'd never heard any of his tales before. They were gripping and original to her ears. Time flew by as she listened to them, and she'd be fast asleep in no time—and stopped jolting awake in the middle of the night. Her favorites were "Cinderella" and "Snow White."

This may have been around the time Beta began chasing Shadow with her eyes.

She noticed she was spending more and more time around him. At first, she observed him with a timid gaze. But after a year had passed, Beta was attached to him at the hip.

Shadow was indispensable to the Shadow Garden—absolute strength, knowledge, and wisdom. His unconditionality comforted Beta. Soon enough, she found he'd become a necessity to her, too.

She realized her doubts had disappeared somewhere along the way.

Without Shadow, Beta would have been killed for being possessed.

She'd been disowned by her family, chased out of her home country, and this series of tragedies made Beta slow in processing her new situation. She'd lost too much to notice her gains.

With her skepticism gone, Beta was able to realize something: Shadow had given her a new life and strength.

She could feel this truth swelling in her heart.

Beta had found a reason to fight.

She began keeping a journal to write about him every day—for her to keep in touch with her memories and feelings, for her to never doubt anything again.

Beta had found a reason to live.

At first, she'd jotted down words and adjectives, but she noticed it had turned into sentences, and that flourished into a story somewhere along the way.

The faint sound of movement brings Beta back to reality. She unsheathes her sword before approaching the loading deck and peers under the wagon.

"Eek!"

She locks eyes with a young soldier about her age.

He panics and drags himself out of the confines, trying desperately to escape.

He didn't know a thing when he chose to guard the carriage hauling the possessed—and he will know nothing in death.

"S-stop…!"

Beta swings her sword down without hesitation, and blood squirts out of his neck as he sprints for his life.

He staggers a few more steps before collapsing to the ground. Swiping the blood spatter off her cheek, Beta gazes at the night sky, where a full moon peeks out from between the clouds. Under the moonlight, she smiles innocently—as if she's a lovely flower fraught with danger in the night.

Beta has no doubts.

If it would make him happy, she would even walk down the path of evil.

The Eminence in Shadow

stly can't remember what catalyzed this desire.

now is I've admired shadowbrokers for as long as

emember.

a certain anime? Or was it a manga—or a movie?

guess it doesn't matter. I was all in for anything that featured a

mind, or an eminence in shadow, as I like to call them. These

ters were never the protagonists or final bosses but were relegated to a role

d the scenes where they flaunted their powers and meddled in the

of others. I've always looked up to the men in the shadows.

ted to be one of them.

All I know is I've admired shadowbrokers for as long as
I can remember.

Was it a certain anime? Or was it a manga—or a movie?
Eh. I guess it doesn't matter. I was all in for anything that featured a
mastermind, or an eminence in shadow, as I like to call them. These
characters were never the protagonists or final bosses but were relegated to a role
behind the scenes where they flaunted their powers and meddled in the
affairs of others. I've always looked up to the men in the shadows.
I wanted to be one of them.

Think of children who worship their favorite superheroes.

That was me but with master puppeteers.

Assuming the Role of a Side Character at School!

Chapter 2

The Eminence in Shadow

Chapter 2

I turned fifteen and started attending the Midgar Academy for Dark Knights at the royal capital. This academy is known as the crème de la crème of schools on our continent and where promising knights gather not only from this nation but all over the world. I kept my grades on the *meh* tier to blend in with the crowd and my eye on the protagonists of my dreams.

One of them is Princess Alexia Midgar, the biggest fish of them all.

Honestly, even a chimpanzee would know she's on the top tier.

I've heard there's an ultra-famous super–big shot named Princess Iris Midgar, but she already graduated, to my chagrin.

Anyway, I'll have you know that I unlocked a special event with Princess Alexia…er, I mean, my punishment for losing a game. Yeah, you've heard that right. I'm about to take part in your ye old punishment of confessing to a girl.

Which brings us to the rooftop of the school. I face Princess Alexia from a distance.

Her platinum hair is cut straight across at her shoulders, and her red eyes are almond-shaped and, um, pretty? And she looks all aloof with her perfect face. It's like *Yeah, yeah, we get it already. She's gorgeous. Yeah, whatever.*

I hate to break it to you, but I'm bored of beautiful women, thanks to Alpha and company. I prefer a touch of ugliness. It makes you unique, you know.

Anyway, I'm not the only reckless challenger who's gone after Alexia. It's been two months since the beginning of school, and more than a hundred schmucks have already tried to win her over.

And all of them were met with one bitter phrase: "I'm not interested."

I mean, I get it. I'm guessing she's got a political marriage or something lined up for her when she graduates. I bet she's trying to say she doesn't have time to engage in child's play.

That said, the aristocratic students in love with her share the same fate—political marriage and all. But I think that's why they want to have a little fun while they're still in school.

Well, it doesn't matter either way. In the end, it's nothing but the amusement of those who know nothing of the shadow realm.

And it's my duty as a background character to join in on this charade. To get brutally rejected by the most popular girl in school? I can't think of a role more fitting for an extra. If I can get through this event and play the role of a real loser, I will become my ideal and take another step toward becoming a hidden mastermind.

I stay up all night to prepare for this moment. *What should I say? How should I confess to her…?* This is gonna be the greatest confession by a minor character of all time.

Choosing the right words is a given. But I take it a step further by experimenting with articulation, pitch, and vibrato. I finally master the ultimate confession.

On this day, at this very moment, I'm standing on the battlefield of a lifetime.

Ready, fight.

It's a momentous battle for a background character.

Sure, shadowbrokers have their own way of combat, but fighting as a side character creates a breed of its own.

Which means I'm gonna pull out all the stops as one.

I'm secure in my decision when I turn toward her.

Princess Alexia… She's standing there looking all high-and-mighty, but I could unsheathe my sword and detach her neck from her torso in a heartbeat. *You're a human like the rest of us.*

Watch closely.

I present to you, the greatest confession in the world!

"Pwinshesh A-A-A...Alexia."

Did you hear how I stuttered on the *A-A-A*? And that staccato? I threw in a bit of vibrato, changed pitch midway through, and added a lisp to *Pwinshesh* to give a convincing performance.

"I—I love you...!" I lower my eyes to evade her gaze, making sure my knees are knocking against each other. "W-will you be my girlfriend...?"

I choose to go with your average confession—cliché, if not boring. But I let my pitch and tone go hog wild. And that upward lilt at the end? It shows my complete lack of confidence.

It's perfect...!

This is the performance of my dreams. I'm satisfied! I'm completely satisfied!

"Sure."

"Huh?" I'm pleased with myself and just about to leave when I experience an auditory hallucination. "What did you just say?"

"I said...sure."

"Um, okay."

Something's not right.

"L-let's head back to campus together."

From there, I walk Princess Alexia to her dorm room. After a "See you tomorrow" with a smile on my face, I head to my own room, bury my face in my pillow, and scream at the top of my lungs.

"When did I become the protagonist of a rooooooooooomcom!!"

"It's weird, right?!"

"Bizarre."

"Absolutely bonkers."

It's the next day. I'm having at lunch in the cafeteria and just told my two friends about yesterday. We're all in agreement: There's definitely something strange going on.

"No offense, but Princess Alexia is way out of your league. If she said yes to me? I'd still think it was fishy. Right?"

That's Skel, the second son of the Baron Etal. He's slim and tall, and though it seems he cares about his outer appearance, he has zero style. If you look at him from far away, he could trick you into thinking he's hot. Erm, maybe not. I take that back.

Either way, Princess Alexia is way out of Skel Etal's league, too. I know this for a fact, because I consider him my "minor character" friend.

"If Cid's good enough for her, I bet I would've been good enough, too. Gah, I really should have confessed to her earlier."

That's Po, the second son of the Baron Tato. He's short and somewhat stocky. You know how there's one potato-esque guy on every baseball team? That's basically him.

It doesn't matter if you look at him from afar, from up close, or from any and all angles. With his looks, he could never scam anyone into thinking he's cool. It goes without saying that he has absolutely no chance with Princess Alexia. After all, he's your cold, hard background character.

Oh, and by the way, my name's Cid. When I'm playing the part of Cid Kagenou, I'm also playing the part of your average Joe.

"To be honest, it's terrible. I have a feeling she's got an ulterior motive, which freaks me out. Plus, we basically live in two totally different worlds."

"Yeah, I hear you. And unlike me, you're not blessed in the looks department. I'd give it a week before she calls it quits."

"Three days. Just look around you."

I scan the cafeteria and see everyone whispering and observing me.

"Over there! That's..."

"You're kidding! He's super average..."

"It must be some kind of mix-up..."

"Oh, I think he's pretty cute..."

"No way!"

Et cetera.

"I heard he blackmailed her...according to Skel Etal."

"I'll kill that son of a bitch..."

"And make it look like an accident during practice..."

"If I don't do it now, I'd bring shame to mankind..."

And the like.

I've got pretty good ears, and I'd caught almost all their chatter. I take a moment to glare at Skel.

"Hmm? What's up?"

"Nothing."

I guess friendships between minor characters can be fickle and fleeting.

"But seriously, what do I do? It'd be weird if I mentioned breaking up when I just confessed my love for her."

And it would break character to dump a princess—though I guess people in this role wouldn't date them in the first place.

"Come on, give it a try. If you're lucky, you might make some nice memories," Skel encourages with a sly grin.

"He's right. Let's say this is all a misunderstanding. You still get to date a *princess*. Don't waste your time dealing with bullies," Po adds.

"It doesn't work that way."

Even as we waste time now, rumors about me will continue to circulate around the school—meaning I'm getting pushed further and further away from my existence as an average nobody.

"But now that you two are actually going out," Po muses, "you've gotta stay quiet about losing that game."

"Yeah. I can see things getting messy if word got out. Please don't say anything. I'm looking at you, Skel."

"Me? I'd never say anything!"

"I'm serious."

I sigh as I reach for my daily lunch for broke aristocrats—which costs exactly 980 *zeni*. I'm starting to get annoyed by the vibe of this place. I'm just going to eat as quickly as possible and skedaddle out of here.

Erm, well, that was the plan.

But a group of maids set the lunch course of the super-duper filthy rich—which costs a whopping ten thousand *zeni*—in the seat across from me with marked efficiency.

"Is this seat available?"

Enter Alexia. Ugh, I knew she was here. That's why I was trying to scarf down my lunch.

"P-p-pwease do!"

"Y-y-you can sit here! It's our pleasure!"

Skel and Po respond, basically shriveling into nothing. These are the same guys who were talking big game about how they could date her if they wanted to. Yep, just as expected of my friends.

"Yeah, sure. Go ahead," I say to Princess Alexia, who's waiting for my answer.

"I don't mind if I do," she replies, taking a seat.

"Nice weather we're having." It seems like an obvious way to fill the silence.

"Indeed."

Our innocuous conversation continues, and with the elegant movement of her hand, she starts eating her extravagant lunch.

"There's so much food in the super-duper filthy-rich lunch course."

"Yeah. I can never finish it."

"What a waste."

"I would be fine buying a cheaper lunch, but if I don't get the expensive one, the others might feel too shy to ask for it."

"Uh-huh, I see. Can I eat your leftovers?"

"Yes, but…"

"Oh, don't worry about being polite around me. I mean, this is the section for low-ranking aristocrats."

Alexia looks baffled as I swipe the meat from her main dish and cram it into my mouth before she can get a word in edgewise.

Oh, it's good.

"Um..."

"Pass the fish."

"Wait...!"

Whoo-hoo, it's my lucky day. Thanks to the princess, I get to fill my stomach, which is blissed the hell out. You might notice that my attitude toward her has changed from yesterday and that I'm acting super-casual around her.

And if you want to know why...

It's 'cause I'm in the middle of Operation: Get Dumped ASAP!

"*Sigh*... Sure, whatever."

"Thanks for the meal. See ya later."

"Halt!"

Dammit. My plan to dine and dash fails, and I reluctantly slink back to my seat.

"I assume you're taking Royal Bushin for your practical elective in the afternoon."

"Yurp."

The academy requires its students to take general courses in the morning and practical electives in the afternoon. The former takes place in set classrooms, but the latter is a mishmash of students from all classes and grades. We're basically allowed to choose one of many weapon arts electives that we feel suits us best.

"I'm in that class, too. I thought it'd be nice to take it together."

"Yeah, no. I mean, you're in section one. I'm in section nine."

Bushin arts is so popular that it has nine different sections, with fifty students in each, divided up by skill level. For now, I'm performing poorly enough to be in section nine, so I can scope things out. I plan to eventually settle for section five.

"No, it's okay. With my recommendation, I got you into section one."

"It's totally not okay. I know that for a fact."

"Would you rather that I enroll in section nine?"

"No, stop. That'd make me look bad."

"It's one or the other. Choose."

"No."

"This is a royal order."

"I'm off to section one."

With that, lunch is over. Skel and Po were completely still from start to finish, basically melting into the background.

"This place is huge...," I marvel the moment I step into the classroom for section one. I can't help myself.

To put it simply, it looks like a ginormous gymnasium. In addition to the standard locker room, it is fully equipped with a shower room, a café, and a maid who opens the entrance, which technically makes it a manually operated automatic door.

As for section nine, we meet outdoors—rain or shine, sleet or snow. There isn't even a door for a maid to open, much less a maid.

To avoid getting bullied by the other students, I hastily change into my uniform and wait for Alexia in the corner for a while.

"Let's loosen up," she suggests as soon as she enters the room in her Bushin uniform.

Think plain cheongsam, one of those tight-fitting dresses you might see in a movie about the 1920s, with a high leg slit. That's the uniform for girls. Hers is black, which indicates she's one of the strongest fighters. In Bushin, each color represents a different level of strength: Black is at the top, and white is at the bottom.

I'm in white, obviously. And since I'm the only one in white in this entire room, I stick out like a sore thumb.

I ignore the stares of other students—70 percent hostile, 30 percent curious—and warm up with some light stretches.

"Interesting," remarks Alexia, mirroring my movements.

In this world, it's common knowledge that it's beneficial to loosen your muscles before working out. But with no how-to guides on stretching, everyone does it in their own way. I mean, if you're a die-hard for sports, you'll hurt yourself if you don't stretch properly. I've heard of others using magic to force their muscles to loosen up, but this still affects their performance.

Alexia is well versed in that sense, which is nice. I mean, I'm a high-maintenance purist when it comes to battle. Like, I won't lose to the average pretentious snob.

We're getting ready when class begins.

"Starting today, we have a new friend joining us," our instructor starts, introducing me.

"I'm Cid Kagenou. It's nice to meet you."

There isn't a hint of friendliness in my classmates' eyes.

Ah, section one. A quick glance around, and I can already spot some VIPs. That hot guy over there is the second son of a duke, and that beauty is the daughter of the current leader of the Dark Knights. Then there's our teacher, who's the fencing instructor for the country. And on top of that, he's a young blond hunk who's only twenty-eight years old.

"Let's welcome him to our class."

With that, we start training, suppressing our magic through meditation first before practicing our swings and going over the basics of swordplay.

Nice, nice. I'm all for reviewing the basics. They're important to know. In section nine, we'd wave our swords for a few seconds and play-fight the whole time. It's nice to see the strongest fighters value their fundamentals. Plus, all the students are skilled. I can say it's a neat environment—and I'm not trying to suck up or anything.

And most importantly, the techniques taught in this class are hyper-logical. It feels great to take part in training that doesn't leave me bored out of my mind.

"Do ya like the Royal Bushin method?" Our hunky blond instructor approaches me.

I think his name is Zenon Griffey.

"Does it seem that way?"

"Yeah, you look like you're enjoying yourself."

"I guess I am."

Mr. Zenon grins in an easy-breezy type of way. "As you know, the Royal Bushin method is a relatively new fighting style, a deviation from traditional Bushin. There was some resistance at first between the traditional supporters and the trailblazers. But thanks to Princess Iris, it's now being recognized as the artistic heir of its traditional counterpart."

"And I hear you're one of the swordsmen who's spread the art throughout the country, Mr. Zenon."

"Yeah, but my contributions are nothing compared to Princess Iris's. In any case, the Royal Bushin method practically raised me, which is why it makes me happy to see others enjoying it, too. Oh, I'm sorry. I didn't mean to interrupt you."

With that, Mr. Zenon goes to check in on the other students. I totally understand his feelings. I mean, I get all giddy when Alpha and the other girls watch me show off my swordplay. I've developed these techniques on my own, which makes me all the more excited when others take them on, too.

"What did you two talk about?" Alexia asks.

"The Royal Bushin method."

"Hmm. We're going to spar next. Let's pair up."

Sparring is basically a form of light training where we review techniques, reversals, and battle processes without actually hitting our opponent.

"Aren't you too strong for me?"

"It'll be fine."

We pick up our wooden swords and start exchanging blows.

I swing, and she blocks.

She strikes, and I guard.

We don't hit each other, moving at a sluggish pace, and skimp on magical energy. All around us, the other pairs are locked head-to-head in all-out fights, blasting each other with spells. But to my surprise, Alexia is matching my pace.

No. That's not it… This is normal for her. After all, the purpose of this activity is to review our strategies, meaning that speed and power are pointless. Alexia is focused on this goal—and that alone. I can tell by the way she handles her sword.

This entire country sings the praises of Princess Iris, Alexia's older sister—brilliant and fiendish, the strongest combatant in the kingdom. On the other hand, they don't have much to say about Alexia. She possesses magic and forthright techniques, but she's inferior to her sister. That's what people generally say when talking about Alexia.

But as I spar with her, I think she's good. She adheres to the basics and grasps the foundations of combat, though it feels uninspired.

Yeah, it's run-of-the-mill. But that's the fruit of her labor: Her swordplay is polished, refined, and devoid of all excess. That's the proof that she's mastered the basics step-by-step.

Delta, you could learn a thing or two from her, I think, engaging in a fake conversation with a certain hybrid beast—one whose swordsmanship I find hard to forgive.

"Your swordplay isn't bad," Alexia notes.

"Thanks."

"But I don't like it."

She likes lifting me up to bring me down.

"It's like I'm watching myself fight. Let's stop here for today."

She begins packing up, leaving it at that. Class is over.

Never in my wildest dreams did I expect to get through this elective without a hitch. If I can just get my stuff together, change, and book it to my dorm room, I might be able to…

"Hold it."

My bubble bursts.

Alexia drags me by the nape of my neck.

"This is your answer, I'm guessing," observes Mr. Zenon, who's standing in front of me for some reason.

"I've decided to go out with him."

"You can't keep running forever," he warns, narrowing his eyes.

"I'm just a kid. This situation is too grown-up for me," Alexia replies, following it with a pompous burst of laughter.

This is enough for me to figure out how I could get into this section and why she's chosen to go out with me. Watching their cutscene play out and melting into the background, I pray these two protagonists won't drag me into their drama.

"I know that Mr. Zenon is your fiancé and that you're pushing the onus on me." I confront Alexia after school behind the academic building.

"He's not my fiancé, just one of the suitors," Alexia corrects, looking all calm and composed.

"It's the same thing."

"It's not. He keeps pressing the issue as if it's a done deal, and it's stressing me out."

"That has nothing to do with me. I hate to break it to you, but I have no plans to get sucked into this mess."

"You're awfully cold for a lover."

"A lover? Come on. You just needed a red herring to take the fall for you. Isn't that right?"

"Fine. But that goes for both of us," she quips, a devious smile spreading across her face.

"Both of us? What the hell are you talking about?"

"Playing dumb, huh? Mr. I-confessed-to-a-girl-as-a-punishment, Cid Kagenou." Her grin broadens.

Okay...hold up. Let's chill out for a sec.

"Oh, to play with the heart and purity of a maiden," she laments. "How cruel."

Says the girl without a trace of purity in her entire body. Alexia lets a few fake tears fall from her eyes.

It's okay. I'm totally calm.

"I have no idea what you're talking about. Do you have any proof?"

Right, evidence first. As long as the guys didn't stab me in the back, it won't matter how suspicious she is of my intentions...

"I think his name's Po. When I approached him, he turned bright red and blabbed everything, including things I didn't ask about. Nice friend you've got there."

I imagine myself beating him into a pile of mashed potatoes to regain my mental composure.

"Are you all right? Your cheeks look all puffy."

"I'm fine. I break into a smile 'cause I'm broken inside."

"Oh. Huh."

"But I'm not as bad as you."

"Hmm? Did you say something?"

"Nothing. What do you want from me...?"

I have no choice but to accept defeat. My fatal flaw is choosing the wrong friends.

"Well..." Alexia crosses her arms and leans against the wall of the academic building. "Let's keep pretending we're together for now—until that man gives up."

"I'm only the son of a baron, you know. I'm not enough to stop him."

"I know. I just need to buy time. I'll figure something out."

"And I don't want you to put me in harm's way. I mean, the dude is a master swordsman. If things don't work out, I'm gonna get my ass handed to me."

"Stop whining," Alexia snaps before fishing some coins out of her pocket and scattering them onto the ground. "Pick them up," she orders.

Each coin is worth ten thousand *zeni*, and I count at least ten on the floor.

"What? Do I look like I'd be swayed by cash?" I ask from all fours, carefully retrieving the coins one by one.

"You do."

"You're damn right."

Eleven...twelve...thirteen coins... Oh, snap! I found another one!

Just as I extend my hand to collect the last coin, she stomps on the change with her loafer.

I look up at Alexia, and her red eyes bear down on me.

I can see up her pleated skirt.

"Are you going to do as I say?" she asks with a grin that oozes wickedness.

"Of course." I smile from ear to ear.

"Good dog."

Alexia pats my head before briskly walking away with her short skirt billowing behind her. I wipe her footprint from the coin and gently place it in my pocket.

Even as I attend the academy, I continue cutting down on sleep to keep training, but this fake courtship with Alexia is really sucking up my time.

"Come with me."

With this order, I'm dragged into the classroom for section-one students in the Royal Bushin elective at the wee hours of the morning. We're the only ones here. The sun is streaming into the room, and it's peaceful.

It's time for morning practice.

Alexia swings her sword, and I follow suit next to her.

She's very serious when it comes to practice. It's the one thing I don't mind about her. We never speak, just practice in absolute silence, and I'm not annoyed about spending time with her—for once in my life.

"Your swordplay is strange," Alexia comments. "You've got the basics down. That's it, but…" She pauses.

I'm obviously subduing my strength, magic, and abilities as I slice through the air. Which leaves me with the fundamentals.

"…But I can't take my eyes off it."

"Thanks."

I can hear the birds chirping outside, but I know they aren't whistling a tune to themselves. It's a war cry to claim their territory, which means they're really duking it out.

"But I still don't like it," Alexia adds.

We don't speak after that. We just keep practicing.

Two more weeks pass, and I'm somehow managing to survive as Alexia's "boyfriend."

Every once in a while, the other students will bully me, but it's nothing I can't handle. I'm just relieved Mr. Zenon hasn't beaten the living shit out of me or availed himself of any quick and savage tricks to erase me from existence.

In fact, Mr. Zenon is polite to the two of us during class, instructing us as if he and I don't have beef with each other. He doesn't approach me to shoot the breeze anymore, but I would say he's a proper adult who can keep his work and private life separate.

And then there's the royal pain in my ass.

"That jerkwad pisses me off. Thinks he's all that just because he's all right with a sword."

Alexia acts nice to his face, but behind closed doors, she's a foul-mouthed tornado.

"Uh-huh, yup. Whatever you say."

I've turned into a yes machine. By this point, I know disagreeing only wastes time.

"Pooch, I'm guessing you saw his fake-ass grin, too."

"Yep, yep. I saw it all right."

We're on our way home after school.

Of late, we've gotten into the habit of taking a small detour down a quiet path through the forest on the way back to her dorm. I spend the whole time yessing her and seldom retain more than 10 percent of our conversations.

It's sunset as we walk at an excruciatingly slow pace down the road. It should take ten minutes to walk its entirety, but it always takes us half an hour.

There are days it takes so long that the stars come out, but I keep my cool. There are days when I feel like telling her to talk to a brick wall, but I show some self-restraint then, too.

Patience, patience, patience. But there's one thing I feel I have to say.

"Hey, can I ask you something?"

"What is it, Fido?" Alexia sits on her favorite stump and crosses her legs.

Don't just sit there. Let's get a move on, I don't say as I sit down beside her.

"What don't you like about Mr. Zenon? Objectively speaking, he seems like a home run of a husband."

"Have you been listening to me at all?" Alexia asks, slightly vexed. "I hate everything about him. His very existence."

"I mean, he's a hot expert swordsman with titles, prestige, money—not to mention a good work-life balance and personality. And he's popular with the ladies."

Alexia snorts. "Yeah, on the surface. Anyone could pretend. Take me, for an example."

"Wow, I'm suddenly completely convinced."

Now that she mentions it, she's super-popular because she's the master at wearing a mask in front of others.

"That's why I don't judge people by their looks."

"Then what do you look at?"

"Their flaws." Alexia smiles smugly.

"What a negative approach. It suits you perfectly."

"Why, thank you. And just so you know, I don't mind you, even though you've got nothing going for you."

"Thanks. I've never received a compliment that's made me feel worse."

Alexia chuckles dryly. "You're scum through and through, and I like it that way. It's also why I can't stand our instructor."

"What are his flaws?"

"He doesn't seem to have any."

"Sounds like a keeper."

"I told you before: Perfect people don't exist. I bet he's either a big fat liar or totally messed up in the head."

"I see. Thanks for that totally arbitrary and biased answer."

"You're welcome, my flawed pooch. Now fetch!" Alexia tosses a coin into the air, and I scramble to retrieve it.

Whoo-hoo! Another ten thousand zeni. *I'm gonna catch 'em all.*

I shove the coin in my pocket and return to Alexia, who's clapping her hands in delight.

"Good doggy." She rubs my head.

Patience, I tell myself.

"Ooh, you hate this so much," she observes as she vigorously tousles my hair.

I take this opportunity to remember she's the worst.

"I can see the disgust in your face," Alexia notes.

"I'm letting you see it."

She giggles and gets up. "All right. Let's head home."

"Yep, yep."

"And, Fido, note that I'm going to lodge my wooden sword into that damned instructor's face tomorrow. Make sure you're watching."

This compels me to ask another question.

"Would you seriously do that?"

"What do you mean?" she replies, turning back to glare at me.

I think I'm butting into something when I should stay in my lane. But I can't let this slide.

"Mr. Zenon is definitely stronger than you but not to the point where you wouldn't be able to fight back."

I like the way she handles her sword. Her skills evolve every day with her efforts, one step at a time. But in an actual fight, there would be too many extra movements. I would hate to see it sully her swordsmanship, especially since I think it's good.

"You make it sound so easy. Even though you're the one wearing white."

"Don't mind me. It's just the ramblings of a white coat."

"Fine, I'll let you know the truth. It's not as easy as you think."

"Hmm?"

"I have no talent. I was born with a significant amount of magical energy, and I've worked hard to get to this point. I think I'm all right now, but I know I don't stand a chance against a true genius."

"Maybe."

"I've always been compared to my older sister, Iris. Everyone expected great things from me. And more importantly, I respected Iris and wanted to be at her level. But I realized I'll never be as good as her. I mean, we weren't born on the same playing field. I tried my best to get stronger. But I'm guessing you already know how people describe my fighting style."

There's a certain phrase that's always uttered when the two sisters are compared.

"The swordplay of an amateur."

"That's right. And yours is, too. How unfortunate." Alexia flashes me a lopsided smirk.

"I don't think it's unfortunate. I like your swordplay."

Alexia reacts by holding her breath for a moment and scowling.

"I've been told that before. By Iris—when she beat me onstage at the Bushin Festival." Alexia curls her lips and imitates her sister: "'I like your swordplay.'

"She doesn't understand me at all. I felt pathetic, and she had no idea. Ever since then, I've always hated the way I fight."

Alexia smiles, but I don't know why. At the very least, I know she isn't happy.

There's something I need to tell her. If I don't say it now, I'll be stabbing myself in the back.

"You know, I'm as apathetic as they come. If there was a catastrophe that wiped out a million people on the other side of the world, it wouldn't affect me. If you went nuts and became a serial killer, I wouldn't be bothered," I say.

"If I lost my mind, you'd be the first person I'd kill."

"But there are certain things I care about. They might be insignificant to others, but to me, they're more precious than anything. I live this life protecting these few things. Which is why I really mean what I'm about to tell you."

One simple phrase.

"I like your swordplay."

After a brief silence, Alexia replies, "So what?"

"Nothing. I guess the main takeaway is that it peeves me when other people tell me what I can and can't like. That's all."

"I see." Alexia pivots on her heels. "I'm heading home alone today."

And then she walks away.

"It's been a while since the three of us have eaten together," comments Po the Traitor.

"That's 'cause he was dining with the princess every day," adds Skel.

"Shit happens," I say.

It's the first time in a long while that the three of us sit together in the cafeteria. Alexia isn't here, which is rare.

"Come on, Cid, cheer up."

"Yeah! Real men don't hold grudges, you know."

"We even bought you the lunch for broke aristocrats today, costing nine hundred and eighty *zeni*."

"Our treat! Let bygones be bygones, and let's be friends again."

"All right already." I let out a heavy sigh.

"Yeah, that's our man!"

"Thanks for forgiving us, Cid."

"Whatever."

"So how far did you get?" Skel asks, holding back his excitement.

"With what?"

"Well, did you *do the deed* with the princess? You've been dating a whole two weeks, so you must've done something."

I know we're about to have a dumb conversation, based solely on the fact that he said "Do the deed."

"We didn't do anything. That would never happen."

"Huh. You're a friggin' wuss. I would've gone all the way for sure."

"Right? I would've smooched her—at the very least."

"I told you. Our relationship isn't like that." I deflect and nod through their conversation indifferently as I chow down.

"Can I have a moment?"

Enter Mr. Zenon, the blond-haired hunk.

"Yes, of course!"

"By all means!"

With that, my two pals melt into the background again.

"Can I help you?" I ask, slightly on guard. I'm wary that he might pull something while Alexia's not around.

"Indeed. You might have heard already, but Alexia hasn't returned to her dormitory since yesterday."

This is the first I've heard of it. I'm guessing she's gone off on a journey to find herself or whatever. The timing seems about right for her age.

"I was searching for her this morning when I found this." Mr. Zenon holds out a loafer in one hand.

It's Alexia's.

"There's evidence of a struggle nearby. The Knight Order is investigating this case as a potential kidnapping."

"No way…!" I shout in torment as I vigorously fist pump in my mind.

Ha! Serves you right, princess!!

"We narrowed the culprit down to the person who last came into contact with her." Mr. Zenon looks me square in the eye. "The Knight Order would like to have a word with you."

I notice the entire Order is in full gear, standing menacingly at the entrance of the cafeteria.

"I'm assuming you'll cooperate, right?"

That's when it hits me.

This ain't good.

The Eminence in Shadow

All I know is I've admired shadowbrokers for as long as I can remember.

Was it a certain anime? Or was it a manga—or a movie?

Eh, I guess it doesn't matter. I was all in for anything that featured a mastermind, or an eminence in shadow, as I like to call them. These characters were never the protagonists or final bosses but were relegated to a role behind the scenes where they flaunted their powers and meddled in the affairs of others. I've always looked up to the men in the shadows.

I wanted to be one of them.

Think of children who worship their favorite superheroes.

That was me but with master puppeteers.

tly can't remember what catalyzed this desire.

now is I've admired shadowbrokers for as long as
emember.

a certain anime? Or was it a manga—or a movie?

uess it doesn't matter. I was all in for anything that featured a
mind, or an eminence in shadow, as I like to call them. These
ers were never the protagonists or final bosses but were relegated to a role
the scenes where they flaunted their powers and meddled in the
of others. I've always looked up to the men in the shadows.
d to be one of them.

Chapter 3

My Official Beginning as a Mastermind in Action!

The Eminence in Shadow

Chapter 3

I was interrogated in a room comparable to a detention cell and released after five days. It's evening now.

"Go on. Scram."

They shove me out of the building and chuck my suitcase behind me. I'm in nothing but my underwear, and I rummage through my suitcase to change and shove my feet into my shoes. It takes me a while to get dressed. I'm guessing it has to do with the fact that all my fingernails were ripped off.

When I get everything on, I heave out a big sigh and start walking. I stand out among the people on the busy street since I'm beaten up and drenched in my own blood.

I sigh again. "Chill out, relax. There's no point getting worked up over every little thing."

I manage to stay calm by blocking the faces of the interrogating knights out of my mind.

"They were just doing their job."

Their punches only left surface-level wounds on my body. If I felt like it, I could grow my missing fingernails back. But I don't, because I'm fully immersed in acting out my role as a nobody.

"Yeah, I'm always cool and collected."

Right. Calm.

I let out another long exhale, and my field of vision clears. I pay attention to my surroundings and sense strange shadows lurking behind me.

"Two of them are tailing me."

The kidnapper hasn't been caught. Which obviously means that the state of Alexia's well-being is up in the air.

Just because I've been released doesn't mean it's all sunshine and roses. They just don't have enough evidence to convict me, and my name hasn't been cleared yet.

I trudge back to my dorm room, pretending to hang my head from exhaustion.

"Later…," whispers a quiet voice.

It reaches my ears, accompanied with the faint scent of a familiar perfume.

"Alpha…?"

But I can't find her anywhere among the city folk scurrying past one another on the main road after sunset.

When I flick the lights on in my dorm room, the silhouette of a girl emerges from the darkness.

"You must be hungry."

Her black suit fits her perfectly, accentuating her feminine curves. She's holding out a sandwich with a thick slab of tuna in her hand from Tuna King, the famous restaurant in the capital.

"Thanks. It's been a while, Alpha. Where's Beta?"

I'm famished after not eating a proper meal in five days, and I devour the sandwich. Beta is the one who's supposed to be on rotation to assist me.

"She contacted me. What a mess." Alpha sits cross-legged on the bed.

There's a nostalgic quality to her shiny golden locks that trail down her back and those blue eyes the shape of almonds. She's grown up since last time.

"Yep." I stuff the last piece of sandwich into my mouth.

"There's water in there."

"Thanks." I chug it from a large glass. "Ahhh! I'm alive again."

I strip off my jacket and shoes and dive into bed.

"Hey, at least change out of your clothes."

"Can't. Gonna go to bed now."

"Don't you know the position you're in?"

"I'll leave the preparations to you."

Alpha is brilliant. She'll prepare the best stage for our performance if I just let her do her thing. Until then, I'm gonna sleep… I mean, save up my energy.

Alpha lets out a frustrated sigh. "I'm sure you already know this, but they're going to think you're the culprit if you don't do something."

"True that."

If the real culprit is never found, I can almost guarantee the next suspect in line will be punished. Especially since this involves the kidnapping of a royal. Someone has to die or else the case will never be closed.

Ya gotta love the Middle Ages.

"Wake up. I've got more sandwiches."

"I'm awake."

Alpha hands them over. "Someone is trying to escalate the situation and frame you as the culprit."

"Huh. Like, I'm gonna be convicted even if they don't do anything?"

"I'm guessing they want to settle this matter quickly, and an unassuming student from a poor noble family is the perfect target."

"Agreed. I would do the same thing."

"We can't trust the Knight Order."

"Has the Cult infiltrated them?"

"Yes, without a doubt. The abductor is a member of the Cult. Their goal is to obtain high concentrations of the blood of the heroes."

The girls are still pretending that there's a Cult—for me. What a great bunch.

"Is she still alive?"

"If she dies, they won't be able to extract any more of her blood."

"True."

"Though I'm not sure why you decided to woo the princess." Alpha glares at me.

"That's not how it happened."

"I'm sure you have your reasons—reasons you can't tell us."

I don't let out another peep and avert my eyes to avoid her gaze. I have no real reason, of course.

"I understand. I know you're struggling with something deep down in your heart."

How do I respond when that's totally not the case?

"But I hope you can trust us even a little bit more. If you told us about this earlier, it wouldn't have gotten out of hand. Don't you agree?"

"Y-yeah."

"It's okay. Our job is to make sure you're covered," she adds with a smile. "Once we solve this case, you're treating me to Tuna King. That last sandwich was supposed to be mine."

"Of course. Sorry for stealing your sandwich, Alpha."

"Don't worry about it," she insists, standing up and heading to the window.

Once she gets it open, she hooks one foot out of the room, wiggling her tiny hips.

"I'll be leaving now. Lay low for a while."

"Got it. What's our strategy?"

"We'll assemble an army. There aren't enough members in the capital. And I believe we should summon Delta."

"You're sending for Delta?"

"She wants to see you."

Gunshot Delta. Otherwise known as Suicide Weapon Delta. Put simply, she's a blockhead who's spent all her experience points on her battle skills.

A little reunion would be nice, I guess. I'm begging that all of them turned out all right.

"I'll let you know the details when the preparations are complete. See you soon."

Alpha flashes me a final smile before yanking on her bodysuit to hide her face and slipping out the window into the night.

"Is that the end of your report?" asks a redheaded beauty.

Her fiery, straight hair reaches to the small of her back, illuminated under the flickering lights of a candle, and her wine-red eyes are set on the investigation papers on her desk. The reporting knight blushes in the presence of her poise and allure.

"Y-yes, Princess Iris. We'll continue our search to the best of our abilities."

Iris nods, cuing him to take his leave.

When the door clicks closed behind him, Iris is left alone with a handsome man with blond hair.

"Marquess Zenon. Thank you for your cooperation."

"The incident took place on school grounds. I was responsible for keeping her safe, and more importantly, I'm worried about her well-being..."

He lowers his eyes and bites his lower lip in frustration.

"You had to attend to your duties as an expert swordsman. No one blames you. And we don't have time to point fingers right now. We need to focus on getting Alexia back safe and sound."

"I suppose you're right..."

"Another thing." Iris stops speaking for a moment and snaps the report closed. "Is it true that this Cid Kagenou is most likely the perpetrator?"

"I don't want to believe one of our students could be the culprit, but based on the circumstances, I have to say I find him suspicious...though I don't think he's strong enough to overpower Alexia in a duel." Mr. Zenon tacks on the last bit, carefully choosing his words.

"Which means he either had an accomplice or drugged her. But he didn't crack during interrogation. Do you really think it's him?" Iris asks.

"I can't say for certain. But I want to believe him."

Iris nods and narrows her eyes. "I have my most trusted knights surveilling him. We'll wait for the next report."

"I pray for Alexia's safety." Mr. Zenon offers a bow before taking his leave.

Just as he opens the door, a young girl skids through it into the room.

"Your Highness! Please listen!"

"Claire! What are you doing here? Excuse us, we'll be leaving!"

Mr. Zenon grabs the girl with black hair, Claire Kagenou, attempting to push her out of the room.

"Marquess Zenon, who is she?"

He halts. "She's..."

"Claire Kagenou! I'm Cid's older sister!"

"Claire! Sh-she's currently one of our top students, and she's shadowing the members of the Knight Order."

"I see... All right. I'll listen."

"Thank you so much!" Claire exclaims, approaching Iris and pleading her case. "My brother would never kidnap Princess Alexia! This must be a mistake!"

"The Knight Order is taking every precaution in its search to avoid any mistakes. It hasn't been confirmed that your brother is the criminal."

"Yes, but if no one finds the real culprit, he'll take the fall!"

"Our knights are carefully investigating the matter. I can assure you that no one will be wrongfully convicted."

"But!"

"Claire!" Mr. Zenon warns, stopping Claire from desperately pressing Iris any further. "Settle down. I know how you feel, but any more would be an insult to the Knight Order."

"Ksh...!" Claire lets out before glaring at Zenon and then Iris. "If anyone lays a hand on my brother, I'll...!"

"That's enough!!" Mr. Zenon cuts her off and yanks her out of the room.

Slam.

Iris lets out a sigh, staring at the closed door behind them.

"Huh. We feel the same way about our respective families...," Iris murmurs. "Alexia, I hope you're all right..."

The two sisters used to be close, but somewhere along the way, they started drifting apart. In fact, they haven't spoken in years, and Iris knows they may never again.

"Alexia..."

Iris shuts her wine-red eyes and lets a single tear trail down her face.

When Alexia opens her eyes, she finds herself in a dimly lit room with no windows and a candle as the only source of light. A heavy door is embedded in the stone wall before her.

"Where am...?"

She doesn't remember anything after saying good-bye to Fido on her way home from school.

Upon shifting her body, Alexia hears the clang of metal striking metal and looks down to see her limbs bound to a low table.

"A magical restraint..."

That means her magic is being subdued, and it might be tough for her to escape on her own.

Who brought her here and for what purpose? She goes down the list of possibilities: Abduction, blackmail, human trafficking... There's no definitive answer. Though Alexia may not be the heir to the throne, she knows she has enough leverage as a princess to attract criminals.

That said, she has too little information to figure out the current situation.

She takes a step back. A new thought pops into her mind.

Is Fido okay?

Yeah, Fido. An asshole of a friend. But she likes him for speaking his mind without fear.

If he's dragged into this mess, his life would be... Alexia stops herself from finishing that thought, shaking her head to clear it before scanning the room.

A stone wall, a steel door, a candlestick, and...something that looks like a black pile of trash. That heap is chained up for some reason, seated beside her.

Alexia is staring at it curiously when she thinks she sees it move slightly.

It's breathing—something in tattered clothes.

"Can you hear me? Can you understand—...?!"

The being turns to look at her.

It's a creature.

Alexia has never seen one this malnourished before. She can barely make out its eyes, nose, and mouth in its black, festering face. Its entire body is distorted and bloated, and its right arm is longer than Alexia's legs. In contrast, its left arm is thinner and stumpier than hers, and there is a protrusion in its body as if it is carrying something in its stomach.

The creature is right next to Alexia.

Her hands and feet are chained to the table, but it's only bound by its neck. If it were to just extend its long arm, the monstrosity could potentially touch her.

Alexia hushes her breath, averting her eyes to avoid provoking it.

She's being observed.

There is a long pause that seems to freeze time...and then its chains begin to rattle.

Alexia shifts her gaze to the side, and the creature is lying facedown as if it has fallen asleep. She heaves a huge sigh of relief.

It isn't long before the door opens.

"Finally. I've finally got you." A lanky man in a white coat enters the room.

His cheeks are sunken, his eyes caved in, and his lips cracked. The little wisps of hair left on his thinning head are slicked down with the oil from his scalp, from which wafts a dreadful smell.

Alexia calmly watches the man.

"Royal blood, royal blood, royal blood."

Royal blood.

As the man in the white coat repeats this phrase, he retrieves a device equipped with a thin syringe. Maybe he's planning on drawing her blood. The castle doctor took it many times before.

But she doesn't know why this man would kidnap a princess for her blood.

"May I ask you a question?" Alexia asks coolly.

"Hmm, hmm?" A strange gurgle emerges from the man.

"What will you use it for?"

"Y-y-you have the blood of a demon. I'll use it to resurrect them in the modern day."

"I see. Pretty neat idea you've got there."

Although she can't understand what he's trying to say, she's very aware he's gone completely mad and realizes he must be motivated by religion—or something.

"Hey, I'll have a hard time staying alive if you take too much blood. I'm not ready to die, you know."

"Heh-heh-heh… I kn-know. I want all the blood you can give me. I'll siphon bit by bit from you each day."

"Yes, please do."

As long as he needs her blood, he won't kill her. Which is why she keeps docile and doesn't try to resist. For the time being, she decides to wait to be rescued instead.

"Th-th-this wasn't supposed to happen. I blame those morons for all this."

"Uh-huh, I hate idiots, too."

She stares at the man in the white coat as she mumbles under her breath, "Because dealing with them wears me out."

"They destroyed my…my laboratory. It all started with that dumbass Grease."

"Uh-huh, dumbass Grease is the one who started it."

"And then they kept coming and coming and— Aaaghh!"

"That's a shame. I'm sorry to hear that."

"Yes! Yes, it is! My research is almost done! If I don't finish it soon, I'll be banished…banished…!"

"That sounds terrible."

"C-curse it all! That good-for-nothing…nothing!"

The man in the white coat approaches the chained creature and punts it as far as its chain will allow. He kicks it over and over, stomping on its body, as the creature all but keeps still, huddling into itself.

"Weren't you going to take my blood?"

"Oh, right. Right. With your blood… With your blood, everything will be complete."

"Good for you."

The man in the white coat readies the device and sets the syringe against her arm.

"With this… With this, it will be complete… I—I won't be banished."

"Don't hurt me."

It'll make me want to clock you, Alexia adds in her mind.

The needle enters her arm, which she watches as though someone else's blood is filling the glass tube.

"Heh-heh…heh-heh-heh…"

When it's full, the man in the white coat lovingly carries it out of the room, and Alexia waits for the door to close before releasing a heavy sigh.

I've prepared everything for this day.

Two days after I'm released from interrogations, I look through the prized mastermind collection in my dorm room and grab everything of potential use.

These cigars…aren't fitting for my age. But this vintage wine…a rare collector's bottle worth nine hundred thousand *zeni* from Pordeaux in the southwest of French. Yes, it's perfect for tonight—when the moon remains hidden behind the clouds. Now, I'll pair it with my finest glassware… This Buitton is the best in French and costs 450,000 *zeni.* And with this antique lamp and that elusive painting *The Shriek*, which I just so happened to stumble upon, on the wall… Voilà. Fantastic.

Oh, my heart is full.

I've hunted bandits and scrounged for coins on my hands and knees, all for this.

Tears of joy stain my cheeks as I gaze upon my bedroom—a product of my superior collection. All I have to do is set up the invitation I just received today and wait.

I will wait for that moment.

Waiting.

Waiting…

And waiting…!

Then…the moment arrives.

I murmur to myself at the same time the girl in ebony enters through the window.

"The time is ripe… The shadows run the world tonight…"

Yes. I've prepared everything for this day…

"The time is ripe… The shadows run the world tonight…"

Those were the words he used to greet his underling, Beta.

He sits in a chair with his legs crossed, his back to his subordinate. It might be unguarded, but Beta knows that it's distant and lives in a world completely separate from hers.

The wineglass in his hand glows in the light of the antique lamp.

It's even clear to Beta, who isn't too familiar with alcohol, that he's casually sipping on one of the rarest, most unattainable wines of all time.

Beta is stunned not only by the luxury items that color his room but also by the painting she spots on his wall. The unobtainable masterpiece *The Shriek*. No amount of cash could ever purchase this work of art. Beta almost asks how he came to possess the painting, but she suddenly realizes it would be meaningless and stops herself in time.

Everything falls into his hands because he is who he is.

That explains it all.

It's only natural for him to own *The Shriek*. In fact, even if one searched every corner of the world, one could never find a more suitable owner for that painting than Shadow.

"A world of shadows. The clouds cascade over the moon tonight. How fitting. For us," Beta adds.

Shadow silently glances at her and places his mouth on the rim of his glass.

"We're ready."

"Uh-huh."

He knows everything. Or perhaps it's his omniscient tone that creates this illusion. Well, the truth is, he actually knows almost everything Beta is about to say.

But Beta continues to speak regardless, as is her duty.

"Under Lady Alpha's command, we've assembled all the people in the area and mobilized them in the capital. There are one hundred fourteen in total."

"A hundred fourteen?"

"—...gh!"

Is that too few?

Considering the strength of the Shadow Garden, she imagined that 114 new members would be more than enough.

But it doesn't take long for Beta to realize she misunderstood him.

After all, these people are supporting characters, and less than 10 percent of them are qualified for the job. He's the star of tonight's show. As sidekicks to bring the main character's story to light, 114 seems outrageously small in number.

"I'm s-sorr—...!"

"You've hired extras...?" Shadow asks, interrupting her, but that last word isn't in Beta's vocabulary. "Never mind. Just talking to myself."

"Understood."

Beta doesn't inquire any further, because she knows his words contain more depth than she could ever fathom, and she has neither the right nor the power to ask for more details.

That said, she can't stop hoping for a day when she'll stand beside him and support his every secret. But until then, she's going to keep these feelings hidden.

She continues to speak.

"Our strategy is to launch synchronized attacks against the hideouts of the Fenrir sect in the Cult of Diablos scattered throughout the capital. At the same time, we'll search for traces of Princess Alexia's magic. Once we locate her whereabouts, we'll switch plans and prioritize her rescue."

Shadow nods, silently encouraging her to keep going.

"Gamma will handle tactical commands. Lady Alpha will command the battlefield, and I will serve as her assistant. Epsilon will lead support from behind, and Delta will ambush them, marking the beginning of our entire operation. The troops will be formed by..."

Shadow raises his hand, stopping short her detailed explanation.

He's holding a letter.

"An invitation," he adds, flicking it behind him.

Beta catches the sheaf of paper, which he urges her to read.

"This is..." She trails off, shocked and angered by the crass message.

"Send my apologies to Delta...but this prelude is mine to perform."

"Yes, we'll make sure that happens."

"Come with me, Beta." He turns to her. "Tonight, the world will find out who we are."

Beta trembles with joy upon knowing she gets to fight beside him.

The ransom note brought him to the forest path deep in the woods. Shadow makes his appearance in his school uniform, close to where Princess Alexia was abducted, and Beta covertly lurks a short distance away from him.

It only takes a little while before he senses two energies approaching.

Something flies in his direction, which he catches in one hand and glances at.

"Is this...Alexia's shoe?" he mutters.

And then they appear—two men on the path.

"Hey there, chick magnet. What're you doing with Princess Alexia's shoe?"

"Ooh, and it contains traces of magic. You're the culprit, Cid Kagenou."

Both are in the armor of the Knight Order. There's no doubt they're the ones who interrogated him before.

"I see. That's what you're trying to do."

The men unabashedly sneer at Cid's words.

"If you'd cracked sooner, we wouldn't have had to get in this mess."

"You could've gone through it without getting messed up."

The two wield their swords and brazenly close the distance separating them from Cid.

How stupid... Beta can't find the words to describe their idiocy.

"Okay, Cid Kagenou. You're under arrest for the abduction of a princess."

"Don't fight back. Struggling will get you nowhere."

One of them haughtily chuckles as he thrusts his sword toward Cid.

"Hmm?"

But Cid has stopped the blade with two of his fingers. Then, there's a flash of light as his right foot grazes the man's neck.

Blood subsequently erupts from that exact location.

There's an ebony dagger sticking out of Cid's right shoe.

"AAAH… Agh…augh!!" The knight drops to the ground, clutching his neck.

He'll die in time.

"You bastard!!" His partner panics and tries to slash Cid, but his attack is too simple and careless.

Cid dodges by tilting his head, then literally swipes the man off his feet, leaving him empty below the knees.

"Aaaaaaaggghhhhh!!" shrieks the knight as blood gushes from his thighs, which he clutches. "My…my leeeeegs…!"

He starts crawling away from Cid.

"D-don't think you can get away with hurting the Knight Order, you swine…! I-if we die, you're gonna be the first one they suspect!"

Cid leisurely treads the man's trail of blood and draws closer.

"E-eek…! I-it's over for you…! Over…!" screeches his prey, desperately and fumblingly dragging himself across the ground.

"When dawn breaks…they'll find the corpses of two knights."

"Y-yeah! Come morning, it's game over…!"

The man inches forward. Cid follows his bloody path.

"But you don't have to worry anymore."

It's at that very moment the fool realizes that Cid is behind him.

"Eek!"

There's a flash of light from Cid's right leg.

"Because when dawn breaks…everything will be done."

The man's head is flung into the sky, and Cid turns around, blood raining down on him. Beta shudders at the sight.

But Cid is no longer there in his school uniform.

Instead, there's Shadow, head to toe in ebony. Adorned in an inky bodysuit and boots, he holds a black katana in his hand as his coat sways in the breeze. His hood hangs over his forehead, hiding the upper half of his face. Only the lower half sees light. It's as if he's wearing a magician's mask, where the only real visible parts of him are his mouth and the red eyes peering out from the darkness.

After nearly fainting upon seeing his commanding and arresting silhouette, Beta hastily retrieves *The Chronicles of Master Shadow* from between her breasts and draws a rough sketch of the scene. Next to it, she records his utterings from that day. And voilà. All this takes but five seconds.

On an unrelated note, these drawings and lists of his catchphrases comprise the wallpaper in Beta's bedroom. Writing a new entry in *The Chronicles of Master Shadow* every night before bed brings her one of her greatest joys in life.

The roar of a distant explosion drags her back to reality.

"Is that Delta...? Nocturne has begun. Let's go, Beta."

"O-okay! Coming!"

Beta stuffs the notepad back into her cleavage and dashes after him. And, of course, Shadow is totally unaware that she's done any of that in the first place.

"Eek... What the hell are you? We've done nothing to deserve this!"

A sea of blood.

That's what this is. And there's a man screaming in the middle of it.

It has come unannounced. Without any warning or stating its reasons, it burst through the wall and commenced its slaughter.

Yet another man becomes prey to its black katana blade.

No one wants to fight it. The men wish to make a hasty escape and nothing more. But it is blocking the only exit.

"What have we ever done to you?! Nothing, right?!"

It turns to the man and starts to cackle.

"Eek...!"

From behind its ebony mask, it laughs viciously.

"H-help...!" he sputters.

His body is split down the middle, sliced from the top of his skull to his crotch. Blood bursts from each side as the two halves fall to the right and left.

As it submerges its body in blood, it catches the falling drops tenderly. It might have the appearance of a woman, but the temperament is of a devil.

Upon noticing there are only a few spoils in the area, it extends its weapon, elongating its black blade.

Without exaggeration, the katana literally extends far enough to smash through the wall.

With a mighty swing…

"S-stop…!!"

…it destroys the building and everything in it.

"It's begun."

From atop a clock tower, an alluring elf watches the complete annihilation and fall of a building. It's a joke, almost. The breeze tousles her long golden locks, which glisten in the dark of the night.

"Oh, Delta… She always overdoes it." She sighs, shaking her head.

But she can't undo what's already done. Alpha looks over the capital from the top of the tower.

The entire capital begins moving frantically. Everything commences as planned. And most of the attention is directed at Delta, who just hacked a building to bits.

"I have to give it to Delta for making it easier for the others to start…"

If she could just ignore the victims, she could admit Delta's moves are exceptional.

"Guess I should get going, too," she murmurs.

Alpha hides her face behind a pitch-black mask.

There is something going on outside.

Alexia opens her eyes for the first time in hours.

The only ones who ever enter the room are a female caretaker and the man in the white coat, which gives Alexia nothing to do except sleep on the same table that binds her hands and feet. Neither Alexia nor the creature bother the other, which means they are getting along all right. The clamor intensifies, indicating there's some kind of conflict beyond this room.

Alexia smiles, expecting to be rescued.

"I wonder if they'll crash through the wall all dramatically," she mumbles for no particular reason.

The stress must be getting to her. And even though she knows it's meaningless, she shakes the chains that bind her.

"I'm sorry for waking you."

The creature next to her lifts its head.

"But I think it's best to stay awake. You don't want to miss out on the fun."

Alexia knows it won't answer her, but she talks to it anyway. Boredom can have strange effects on the mind.

It takes a while before the sound of the key unlocking the door echoes throughout the room in a flustered and apprehensive way.

"Shit, shit, shit!!" The man in the white coat barrels into the room.

"Good day to you, too."

"I was so close! So close!!" He ignores Alexia, who is clearly having fun with all this. "Those bastards… They're here!! This is the end! The end…!"

"Give it up. Resistance is futile. If you unchain me now, I'll ask them to spare you," Alexia tells him.

"But no guarantees," she adds quietly.

"Th-those brutes would never let me go scot-free…!! Th-they'll kill everyone…everyone!!"

"The Knight Order doesn't kill without reason. If you don't resist and go quietly, they won't take your life."

A voice in her mind chimes in *Not.*

"The Knight Order? I don't give a shit about them! Th-the fiends will kill everyone, everyone, I tell you!!"

"You're not talking about the Knight Order?"

Then who? Alexia can't imagine anyone else. But then again, she knows it's completely possible he's gone nuts.

"Either way, this is the end for you. Turn yourself in."

"No, no, no, no, no!! N-not until it's complete!!" The man in the white coat claws at his head and shifts his bloodshot eyes toward the creature. "I-I've made a prototype. I-if I use this, even a worthless shit like you might be useful."

He pushes the device with the syringe against the creature's arm.

"You shouldn't do that. I don't have a good feeling about this," Alexia warns, sounding quite serious.

But he obviously just ignores her, shoving the needle in its arm and injecting it with an unknown fluid.

"B-behold! I give you a glimpse of Diablos!!"

"Ooh, how exciting."

The creature begins swelling, its muscles bulging before their eyes, and even its skeletal structure starts to expand. Its right arm, which was long and thick, morphs into a malicious and ominous form. Its fingertips sprout nails as long as human legs. Its left arm appears to be holding something and stays stuck to its body.

It lets out a high-pitched shriek.

"I-incredible! Astounding!!"

"This…is surprising."

But the chains cannot endure the rapid growth of the creature and snap off on their own.

"I told you it was a bad idea."

Splat.

The man in the white coat isn't even spared a final scream of agony before he's crushed by its right arm.

"Well, then."

Alexia and the creature lock eyes.

She studies its movements. Her hands and feet are bound, which means there isn't much she can do. But she can move around a little bit. Plus, she can't stand the thought of dying as a consequence of some idiot's mistake.

The creature swings its right arm.

Alexia twists out of the way as much as she can. As long as her injuries aren't fatal, she can survive...!

"—...gh!"

It avoids Alexia and pulverizes the table that binds her. The impact sends her flying against the wall, where she writhes in pain.

"Augh...!"

But she doesn't have any broken bones or visible wounds and can still move. After checking herself for injuries, she quickly rises to her feet.

But the creature is gone, leaving behind a shattered table and demolished wall.

"Did it...really save me...?"

Even if she hadn't shifted away, its arm wasn't anywhere close to hitting her. Which would mean... Nope, it can't be. Maybe it missed.

"Well, anyway."

Alexia swipes the keys from the man's corpse and removes her magical restraints. With this, her magic can flow free. She stretches once to loosen up, then heads through the wall the creature destroyed.

There is a long, dimly lit hallway before her. Piles of trampled soldiers litter the ground.

"I'll be taking that."

Alexia borrows a mithril sword from a corpse. It's flimsy, but it'll get the job done.

When she goes down the hallway and turns the corner, she sees someone.

"We can't have you leaving on your own."

"Y-you. Why are you here...?" Alexia's eyes widen with fear.

What in the world is going on?

Iris's red hair swirls behind her as she dashes through the capital late at night.

She was told that a building had been destroyed. At first, she thought she'd misheard the news. But as Iris sprints toward the city, half in disbelief, her subordinates keep receiving report after report.

There are many ambushes occurring in the capital simultaneously.

It doesn't take long for her to reach that conclusion. But there's nothing logically connecting the various locations under attack: firms, warehouses, restaurants, private homes of nobles… The crimes must be premeditated, but she can't figure out the goal.

That said, the capital is shaking.

The Knight Order is mobilized in a state of emergency, and they begin evacuating high-profile leaders. Even though it's late, the residents crack open their windows to check what's happening, and there are more than a few onlookers outside. Iris shouts at the meandering residents, telling them to go home, and rushes to the scene.

Something strange is happening. This is in no way a normal incident.

Iris can sense it.

It's right at that moment when a scream reaches her ears.

"M-monster!! Help…!!"

They are shouts from the Knight Order. They aren't too far away. Iris changes directions and books it toward the cries for help. When she turns the corner down a back street to the main road, she spots the monster.

It's a colossal, hideous beast.

With a swipe of the enormous, blood-soaked fingernails on its right hand, it transforms the knights into piles of flesh.

"What is that?" Iris mutters as she dashes toward it. "Stand back!"

With one fluid movement, her unsheathed blade shimmers in the darkness as it slices through the creature's chest.

*　*　*

And completely bisects it.

She cuts down its immense body in one fell swoop.

"Are you hurt?" Iris calls out to the Knight Order and forgets all about the creature as it slowly falls to the ground.

"Princess Iris, you've saved us!"

"That's our princess! She slayed the monster in one stroke!"

The men are unharmed. Almost all the soldiers are completely unscathed. Well, the ones who survived, at least.

"The monster killed eight of our men."

A single hit took them down.

Her red-wine eyes tremble with sorrow when they fall upon the ghastly corpses.

"Gather the bodies and head back. Please inform the lieutenant that..."

"Princess Iris!" shouts one of the knights all of a sudden.

He's standing there, pointing at something behind her, and the other knights try to raise their muted voices.

"What...?!"

Iris turns and strikes without missing a beat.

Her sword collides with the right arm of the creature.

"Ksch...!"

For a moment, it seems as though Iris has been beaten until she quickly releases a huge quantity of magic that effectively blasts its mighty arm. From there, she dives into its bosom, severing its leg, and leaps back to prepare for a counterattack.

In the following second, the monster swings its right arm where Iris had stood and retrieves a few strands of her long red hair.

"Is it regenerating...?"

The injuries from the bisection vanish, and the new wound on its leg is starting to heal.

"Ridiculous... How can it regenerate when Princess Iris sliced it in two...?"

"This can't be..."

"Stay back," Iris calls to the shaken knights as she blocks its next attack. Its moves are quick, powerful, and heavy—but bland.

"It's only a creature, after all."

Iris counters ruthlessly: She slices its arm to pieces, chops off its legs, and beheads it. Successive strikes rain down on the creature, as if to mock, *Try healing from all that.*

She won't let it retaliate. She's the only one attacking.

"Is it *still* healing?"

But the creature survives. In the brief moment Iris stops her assault, it regains its form and swats her away with its right arm.

And then it shrieks into the night sky.

As if in response, rain begins falling from the moonless sky. It drizzles at first but quickly becomes a torrent. White steam rises where the droplets hit the creature's blood.

"This might take a while..."

Iris straightens her posture, preparing for a long fight.

She doesn't think she'll lose. Even now, she never considers that she might see defeat. But it seems this battle is going to require more time.

Iris readies her sword. When the monster finishes healing, she rushes toward it.

The next moment, her sword is knocked out of her hands, accompanied by a shrill sound, and the impact sends pins and needles up her arm.

She glares at a sudden intruder, ignoring the fact that her beloved sword whirls into the distance. The newcomer glances at her.

They stare each other down. The first to break the silence is the interloper.

"Why won't you see it's hurt?"

The uninvited guest is a girl in an ebony bodysuit. Iris can't see her face but notices that her voice sounds young.

"Who are you?" Iris cautiously keeps both the intruder and the creature in view.

"Alpha." After uttering a single word, the girl turns her back to Iris as if she has lost interest in the conversation.

"Wait, what are you planning to do? If you plan to oppose the Knight Order, we won't go easy on..."

"Oppose...?" Alpha cuts in, giggling condescendingly at Iris while continuing to face away from her.

"What's so funny?"

"*Oppose*... I think that might be the most ridiculous word in the world. Opposing an ignoramus would be senseless."

"Excuse me...?!" Iris's magic begins to swell, transforming into a massive wave that sweeps the rain away and forms violent gusts of wind.

But Alpha doesn't even glance in her direction. She stands there unfazed, her back still turned to Iris.

"Play your assigned role as the spectator and keep your eyes on the stage. Don't disturb our performance," she utters before approaching the creature.

From behind, she seems solemn. She's already completely forgotten about Iris.

"Did you just call me a spectator...?" Iris clutches her tingling hands as she glares at Alpha.

"Poor thing. That must've hurt," says Alpha, walking toward the monster. "There is no more pain. No more sadness."

Alpha extends her ebony sword longer than her entire body.

"You don't have to cry anymore."

Then, with a step forward, she slices the creature in two.

No one has time to react.

Iris and the creature can only watch as Alpha bisects it. Everything about it feels natural. There is no bloodlust; it's as if this is the only reasonable solution.

The monster's massive body crashes onto the ground, and white smoke rises from the husk as it gradually shrivels to the size of a little girl. A dagger has fallen from its left hand.

There is a red jewel embedded in it, along with an engraving on its hilt: *To my beloved daughter, Millia.*

"I pray...you achieve peace in your next life."

With that, Alpha vanishes within the white smoke.

A clap of thunder sounds in the distance. Iris is stunned in place. Raindrops run down her hair and fall onto her face.

She's trembling, but she doesn't know why.

"Alexia...," Iris murmurs. She senses that her little sister is at the epicenter of this chaos, and this premonition pushes her forward.

"Alexia, please be safe..."

Iris picks up her sword and starts running. The storm rages on.

"Wh-why are you here?"

When Alexia turns the corner, she sees an all-too-familiar visage.

"Because this is my facility, that's why. I invested thousands of *zeni* into that man. That's all there is to it."

Confidence overflows from the smile stretched across the face of a dashing blond. It's Instructor Zenon.

"That's nice to know. I always thought you were messed up in the head. I guess I was right."

Alexia takes one step back and then two. There's a staircase behind him, and she guesses it's her best bet to escape.

"Huh. Think whatever you want. But I don't mind as long as I have your blood."

"All anyone talks about around here is blood. Is this a research facility for vampires?"

"If that's what you want to think. More or less."

"Skip the explanation. I'm not into the occult."

"Figures."

"I'm sure you're aware, but the Knight Order will be here any minute now. This is the end for you."

"The end? What do I have that can possibly end?" Zenon is still all smiles.

"Your title and reputation will be ruined, and you'll obviously be put to death. I'll be happy to drop the guillotine on your neck."

"You're off the mark. You and I will be escaping through a secret route."

"What a romantic offer. Too bad I can't stand you."

"You're coming with me. With my research and your blood, I'm destined to receive the twelfth seat in the Rounds. I shall bid farewell to my meaningless position as an instructor."

"The Rounds? Is that a group for lunatics?"

"The Knights of Rounds is a gathering of twelve superior knights from my religion. Becoming a member brings me rank, honor, and fortune like you'd never believe. They've already acknowledged my power. All I'm lacking is experience, but my research on your blood should fix that right up."

Zenon melodramatically spreads his arms out and lets out a guffaw.

"Whatever. I'm just sick of all this blood talk," mutters Alexia.

"I would have preferred Princess Iris, but it looks like I'll have to settle for you."

"I'm gonna kill you."

"Oh, excuse me. I forgot you hate being compared to your sister."

"—...gh!"

A forceful swing from Alexia's sword signals the start of their battle. She goes straight for the jugular.

"Ooh, how scary." Zenon repels her attack at the last second and blocks the following strike.

Sparks fly from the colliding blades.

Judging this skirmish merely by the manner in which their swords dance in the air, one might be inclined to say their skills are equally matched.

But the sword bearers wear very different expressions. Alexia angrily glowers, whereas Zenon has a relaxed smile.

And Alexia is the one burning with wrath, sure enough. She clicks her tongue with frustration and backs away.

"You start using shoddy swords the moment I stop seeing you."

Zenon zeroes in on her weapon. She glances at it with a pained expression. The battle has only just started, but her blade is already filled with countless nicks.

"They say the choice of weapon shouldn't matter to an expert." Alexia grimaces and stands her ground.

"I see. If we're talking about experts, I'm sure that's true." Zenon sneers. "But you're mediocre. As a sword-fighting instructor, I guarantee it."

Alexia visibly screws up her face. For a moment, it looks as if her urge to cry is drowned out by pure fury.

"Just watch me. Then you can say if you really think I'm mediocre."

With that, she lunges at him with all the energy she can muster.

Alexia knows. She knows full well she isn't strong enough to beat Zenon, and her flimsy weapon won't last long. But Alexia hasn't spent all those days training with her head in the clouds. In her mission to become as strong as her sister, she's realized her own shortcomings and worked hard to make up for them. She's observed her sister's swordplay more than anyone else and can picture every move with impeccable accuracy.

Which is why it's easy for her to replicate.

"Haaaah!!" It's a stroke reminiscent of her sister's assaults.

"G...!"

For the first time, Zenon's smile vanishes. The sword he's blocked is filled with magic.

The two swords violently clash and repel each other.

They're equally matched...

No.

Alexia might be a bit stronger.

A red line is carved into Zenon's cheek. Visibly taken aback, he looks at the blood he wipes off his cheek.

"I'm stunned."

There is no hidden meaning behind his words.

"I had no idea you were hiding your strength."

Zenon tilts the palm of his hand. He studies it as if checking the color of his own blood.

"I'm going to make you regret looking down on me."

"Pfft." Zenon laughs. "I was certainly taken aback, but you're just a poor imitation, after all. You've a long way to go before you're the real deal." He shakes his head.

"You're asking for it."

"Since we're both here, let me give you a taste of my true power." Zenon readies his sword.

"...g!"

The air changes as Zenon's magic takes on a sharper and deeper quality.

"Let me tell you one thing. I've never shown my true powers to an outsider. I'm about to show you the skills of a true swordsman...of the next generation of the Rounds!"

The air pulses around them.

"That's..."

This isn't in the same ballpark as before.

Alexia has never seen an attack with so much power lurking behind it. Their skills are as hopelessly different as a genius and a clod. He may even rival her older sister.

Alexia doesn't have the means to defend herself against the devastating force of the approaching blade.

Her reaction is involuntary, something that's become a part of her after many years of training.

There is no impact.

The two swords clash, and Alexia's weapon is pulverized into fluttering bits of dust. She feels as though she's watching these sparkling fragments of mithril pass by her from far away.

Somewhere far from here.

Alexia's childhood memories resurface in her mind of times when swinging her sword brought nothing but pure joy.

Her sister is always beside her, and this is a distant memory that should have faded long ago.

"You'll never be as good as your sister."

A single tear falls from Alexia's eye.

"You're coming with me."

Falling from her hand, the measly hilt that was once a sword hits the floor with a dry, metallic clang.

Click, click.

There's a sound coming from the stairwell behind Zenon.

Click, click, click.

Someone is coming down the stairs.

Click, click, click, click.

When the noise ceases, there's a man in an ebony coat in front of them, dressed entirely in black. He has his hood pulled up and wears the mask of a magician.

The man calmly saunters forth, stopping one step outside the range of their weapons.

"The man clad in ebony… So you're the feral dog who dares to nip at the Cult." There's a sharp glint in Zenon's eyes as he glares at the intruder.

"My name's Shadow. I lurk in the darkness and hunt down shadows…" His voice is as deep and as dark as the abyss.

"I see. You seem to have an inflated ego from destroying our smaller facilities, but you haven't even taken down one of our main fighters. You're just a coward who picks on the little guys."

It seems the man who calls himself Shadow is at odds with Zenon. This is good news for Alexia, but she doesn't think this man is her ally.

"It doesn't matter who or what we choose to destroy. It's all the same."

"You're sadly mistaken. The main army of the Cult is here. Today, I'll hunt you down with my bare hands. This is your fate."

Zenon turns his sword to Shadow.

"I'm Zenon Griffey, the next one to fill the twelfth chair of the Rounds. Taking your life will be my achievement for them."

With that, Zenon unleashes a gale of an attack at Shadow.

But Shadow is gone, and he slashes through empty space.

"What the…?!"

The next moment, Shadow is standing behind him. It only takes a second before Shadow takes this position.

Zenon can't move.

As if Zenon has lost track of the time, he stills his sword—even holds his breath—to focus every ounce of his energy on the man standing behind him.

Nobody budges.

That's right. Shadow stands back-to-back with Zenon, arms crossed.

He utters one sentence: "Well then…where are the main troops of the Cult?"

Zenon twists his face in humiliation. He then slices downward from over his shoulder.

But no one is there.

"Absurd…!"

Zenon hears a coat rippling through the air and looks back to find Shadow standing where he originally appeared, as if nothing has changed.

Even Alexia has completely lost track of Shadow as she watches from the sidelines. If this isn't a magic trick or gimmick, then she'd consider him a mastermind… No, he's much stronger than that.

Suppressing his frustration, Zenon slowly turns around.

"I seem to have slightly underestimated your power. While you only destroyed the smaller bases, there were several of them."

This time, Zenon strengthens his magic as he keeps an eye on Shadow. The air undulates from its power. This is more intense than the strike that shattered Alexia's sword.

Shadow is certainly an extraordinary warrior. But Zenon is mightier than the average soldier. A once-celebrated child prodigy, he grew up to win numerous tournaments and climbed the rungs to become a master swordsman. There isn't a knight in the country who doesn't know Zenon Griffey's name.

"I'll show you the power of the one to join the Rounds next term."

So fast…! Alexia barely manages to follow Zenon's sword with her eyes.

The afterimage of the bare blade tears the air and heads straight for Shadow's neck.

"That's one sharp move…"

Somewhere along the way, Shadow raises his black sword and effortlessly blocks Zenon's attack.

"Guh…!"

They're locked in place. Zenon tries to push his way to victory.

But Shadow draws backward, using the swordsman's momentum to send him flying.

"Heh…!"

Just before he slams into the wall, Zenon narrowly manages to tumble on the ground and reposition his sword. But he can't hide his unease.

Neither of them moves.

Shadow has chosen not to move whereas Zenon can't. He feels as if his entire body is being controlled.

"I thought you were going to hit me, Mr. Next-Gen Rounds."

"Nngh…!"

Zenon's face burns a furious red. He's frustrated with his opponent but even more so with himself.

"That's enouuuugh!!" Zenon howls as he executes a sweep attack.

His thrusts forward are as piercing as a squall.

His consecutive strikes are as fierce as a raging fire.

But none of them land.

"Aaaaaagghhhhh!!"

His ferocious roar sounds hollow. It's as if an adult is practicing with a child.

Alexia is in shock watching the fight. She has never seen Zenon reveal this side of himself before. He has torn off his calm smile and mask of integrity, and it's as if they're now out of his reach. The strongest person Alexia knows is her older sister. Even so, Alexia doesn't think her sister would be capable of overwhelming Zenon.

Clang, clang, clang.

The scant noise from their clashing blades echoes through the area and seems almost out of place. It's the exact sound of light practice.

The ebony blade and its white counterpart etch their trajectories through the air.

Alexia's gaze is fixed on this imitation practice session, mesmerized by the black sword. There's a reason her eyes can't stray from it.

"Mediocre swordplay..."

The figure in front of Alexia fights the same way she does.

When Alexia was a child, she had her own idea of perfect swordplay. It isn't about talent, strength, or speed but building up from the basics. Yet others keep comparing her to her sister and mock her for being average, which makes Alexia feel as if she's lost her direction in life.

But despite all her struggles, Alexia never gives up.

And she's just witnessed these unremarkable moves slay the genius Zenon Griffey.

"Amazing...," she mutters admiringly.

Witnessing this, she can see the path he's walked in life. It's a direct result of his serious and unwavering efforts.

Alexia's sister might have the same thought.

"Iris..."

Alexia feels she finally understands her sister's words from long ago.

"Gaghh...d-dammit...!"

Shadow's blade lashes out at Zenon. He's been hit too many times to keep count.

Zenon breathes raggedly as he glares at Shadow. His enraged eyes still haven't accepted reality.

"Y-you bastard! Show me who you are...! Why do you hide your identity when you possess this much power?"

Those with Shadow's strength hold riches and respect within arm's reach—with the potential to be known worldwide.

But no one knows about Shadow's swordplay. Even if he hides his face, those lucky enough to get a glimpse of his swordplay will never forget it. But this is the first time either Zenon or Alexia have seen such phenomenal swordsmanship.

"We are the Shadow Garden. We lurk in the darkness and hunt down shadows. That's the only reason we exist..."

"You're out of your mind...!"

Zenon and Shadow exchange glances.

Alexia is completely excluded from this exchange. She doesn't know why they're fighting or what they're trying to accomplish.

Blood. Creature. Cult. There are many key words to remember.

But Alexia doesn't know what they mean. To her, it all sounds like the ravings of a madman.

But what if? What if it isn't just nonsense? What if there is something going on behind the scenes that Alexia doesn't know about?

"Fine. If you're ready to get serious, it looks like I'll have to answer to your needs."

Zenon produces a pill from his breast pocket.

"With this pill, I shall be awakened and surpass all human limitations. An ordinary human would break under this power and eventually self-destruct. But those in the Rounds are different. Only those who can manipulate this devastating power have the privilege of joining the Rounds."

Zenon swallows the pill.

"I am the Third Awake."

Zenon's wounds instantly begin healing. His muscles tighten up, his eyes become bloodshot, and his capillary vessels protrude. It looks as if he's being crushed by a tremendous force.

"I'll show you almighty power," boasts Zenon, his calm smile returning.

In his current form, there is no doubt Zenon is stronger than Princess Iris.

Alexia thinks Zenon is the strongest being in the world and shrinks back in despair. No…she *would* if she'd never seen Shadow's swordplay.

She doesn't think Zenon's current form is the strongest at all. If fact, she thinks it's something else entirely.

"How ugly…"

"That's ugly…"

Alexia's and Shadow's voices overlap. After all, they're striving to achieve the same type of sword technique, which is why they share the same sentiment.

"Did you just call me ugly?" Zenon's smile slips away.

"Don't call that pathetic form almighty. It's a disgrace to those who are."

"You son of a bitch."

"With borrowed power, you'll never walk the path of the almighty."

This is the first time in this battle that Shadow intensifies his magic. Until now, he's barely used it. It is so exceptionally precise that it's impossible to perceive.

But what is this?

This surge of magic shows itself in the form of blue-violet rays of light. There are hundreds of ultrathin strands. These create a dazzling pattern as they wrap themselves around Shadow like veins.

"It's beautiful..." Alexia is mesmerized by this sight.

She isn't admiring the beauty of the lights, though, but the precision of his magic.

"What is this...?" Zenon is once again shocked.

No one has ever created such beauty through magic.

"I'll show you true almighty power...and carve it into your mind forever."

Magic gathers in the ebony blade and etches out a pattern, starting to form a large spiral. Shadow continues focusing his power.

It seems as if that spiral will swallow everything whole.

A frightening power is absorbed into the black weapon.

"This is me at my peak." Shadow readies his blade in the lunging position.

This stance is only to strike down an enemy.

"S-sto..."

Is the ground trembling? Or the air? Or Zenon himself?

No, it's everything.

Everything is rippling.

Alexia notices that she's shaking, too. It isn't out of fear, though, but joy.

That's the final destination.

That...swordplay is the strongest.

"Watch closely…"

Draped in light, the ebony blade pulls back…

"Hidden Technique: I AM ATOMIC."

…and releases.

All sound is lost.

A torrent of light shoots past Alexia and engulfs Zenon's body. It penetrates everything, consuming the walls and the earth, blasting upward into the night sky.

Then it explodes.

As patterns of light are etched into the night sky, the entire capital assumes a blue-violet hue.

From impossibly far away, the delayed blast ripples across the city, sweeping away the rain clouds, shaking the ground and the private residences, before passing.

All that's left is a full moon and the beautiful night sky full of stars.

Zenon has been vaporized. He doesn't even leave behind a single speck of dust.

The large hole blasts though the wall all the way aboveground.

And then…Shadow flings open his coat and slips into the night.

Once…there was a man who challenged nuclear power and trained his body and mind to hone his techniques.

But it remained far beyond his reach.

And then, after many hours of exhaustive training, he finally found the answer.

Q: How can I withstand nuclear power?

A: Become nuclear power.

From this, the esoteric technique I AM ATOMIC was born. And its power is most certainly comparable to a weapon of mass destruction!

How long did time stand still? Alexia suddenly notices someone calling her.

"Alexia… Alexia…!"

The person gasps for air and shouts from far away. It's a voice she instantly recognizes.

"Iris… Iris…!" screams Alexia, dashing out through the large hole in the wall to the outdoors.

"Alexia! Alexia!!" Iris hurries toward her.

"Iris… I—I…gh."

Alexia is embraced before she can tell her sister she's unharmed. Iris is soaking from head to toe, and her body feels chilly and warm at the same time.

"I'm so glad you're safe… I really am." Iris hugs her sister tightly.

With some hesitation, Alexia wraps her arms around Iris's back.

"I'm sorry. I must be cold."

Alexia shakes her head against her sister's chest. Tears flow from her eyes and won't stop coming.

Two students stand on the roof. It's early in the summer. One is an attractive girl with silvery-white hair. The other is an ordinary boy whose hair is black.

"This incident has been resolved on the surface, but I can sense something brewing behind the scenes. Iris is preparing to dispatch a special brigade, and I plan to help her. So we're only just getting started," says the girl.

"All in moderation," adds the boy.

"Which means you've been cleared of the charges. I really dragged you into that mess."

"Don't worry about it."

A gust of wind passes between them, and her skirt billows to reveal her white legs.

"It's hot as balls out here. Can we go inside?"

The midday sun is beating down on them, and two shadows extend from their feet. They can hear the distant voices of the cicadas chirping.

"Wait. There's two things I have to say."

"Here?"

"Here," she confirms, squinting and looking up at the blue sky. "First, I want to give you my thanks. You said you liked my swordsmanship, right? Well, I know I'm late, but I really appreciate it."

"No problem."

"I finally like it. Not that I attribute that development to you."

"Did you really have to throw in that last bit?"

"It's the truth."

They lock eyes, and he's the first to look away.

"Anyway, if you've learned to like your swordplay, that sounds good to me."

"Yeah, it is." The girl smiles.

"So what's the second thing?"

"We've pretended to date until now, but Instructor Zenon died in that incident."

"Which means I'm freed from my duties."

"But I do have one proposition." The girl looks sort of uncomfortable as she searches for the right words.

"If you're all right with it..." Her red eyes dart around, and her voice softens ever so slightly. "Maybe we can do this a little while longer?"

The boy beams at her.

"No thanks," he answers, flipping her off.

The girl unsheathes her sword in one fluid motion.

That night, a student discovers a large pool of blood on the rooftop.

Despite the heinous amount, there's no corpse in the vicinity. Even when the students and school authorities investigate the matter, there are no wounded or missing persons, and the case is never solved.

Subsequently, this is dubbed the Incident of the Corpseless Murder and considered one of the seven wonders of the school.

One day, out of the blue, Alexia asks her older sister something odd.

"Can you please tell me what kind of apology guarantees forgiveness?"

Iris frowns when she hears the question.

What does she expect from me? She tells Alexia the obvious: "There is no such thing."

Which is common sense, but all of it goes in one of her disgruntled sister's ears and out the other.

"I hate apologizing to begin with," complains Alexia, turning away, at which point Iris throws in the towel and calls it a day.

But Iris is fired up by a sense of duty to do something to help her sister.

From what she gathers, her silly sister annoyed someone close to her. The problem is she hasn't made up for it yet.

Iris realizes this is the first time her sister has ever asked her how to apologize.

Alexia always says sorry when she does something wrong. Of course, this is a superficial apology with no real emotion, but others sharing shallow relationships with her are none the wiser. Until now, Alexia has gotten along just fine.

But if she's asking how to apologize, that means she isn't referring to a fake acquaintance but to a friend.

That little sister of hers has made a friend.

Iris's heart bursts with happiness, a hint of loneliness, and an overwhelming sense of duty.

But telling Alexia will only cause her to rebel. Iris contemplates this situation all night but ultimately can't come up with a good solution.

To start things off, Iris is very direct in conversation but has almost no social grace, as opposed to Alexia, who doesn't like to confront others. Even if Iris suggests something, she knows Alexia won't lend an ear, saying something like "*I'm getting goose bumps from being so uncomfortable*," and that will be the end of it. In every way, the sisters are natural-born opposites.

That's why Iris decides to rely on a certain rumor.

On a rare day when both sisters have spare time, Iris invites Alexia to a department store that's been the talk of the town.

"Iris, what is this place?"

"It's called Mitsugoshi. I think it's all the rage in the capital. I heard they sell some tasty treats."

"Treats? I don't hate that, but…" Alexia looks unamused.

Seeing her sister's expression, Iris panics. "H-hey, I hear girls are really into this new snack called chocolate. Maybe you'd want to give it to someone as a gift!"

Alexia stares coldly at Iris.

"F-for example, a new friend. I bet it'd make them happy."

Iris is very bad at hinting at things. It's painfully pathetic to see her try to force a smile.

"All right, I get the idea. Let's go inside," Alexia suggests, looking terribly bored. "Wait, we can't go in yet. Just look at the line."

A crowd has formed in front of Mitsugoshi, snaking around in a long line in a frenzy.

"We'll cause more trouble for them if we stand in it," she adds.

As if on cue, a member of the staff immediately approaches them.

"Princess Iris and Princess Alexia. Thank you for coming. Welcome."

The woman in a blue uniform politely bows and leads the pair inside. A quick look around shows the two princesses have attracted a lot of attention from the crowd.

"I see," Iris says with a nod. Alexia sighs at her sister.

They pass by the packed shops before they're escorted to a quiet corner of the mall. According to their guide with the dark-brown hair, she's taken them to a special boutique for their most honored customers.

The two princesses find the simple yet tasteful decor of the boutique refreshing, especially because they're accustomed to ornate designs and decorations. Every new and unique product brings a sparkle to Alexia's once-apathetic eyes.

A stunning blue-haired elf appears before them.

"Thank you for your patience. I'm Luna, the president of Mitsugoshi, Ltd. Here is our newest product, chocolate."

A brown, bite-size morsel is placed in front of Iris and then Alexia.

"This is called a chocolate truffle. We've only just put it on the market."

"A truffle…?"

"It doesn't look very appetizing," Alexia comments, sounding indifferent.

"B-but it has a lovely aroma," interjects Iris, immediately trying to make amends for her sister.

"If you'd like, please try a sample," Luna responds with a confident smile.

"Why, thank you."

"If you insist."

The moment they pop the samples into their mouths, their faces light up.

"This is…very sweet. A complex flavor profile. I feel like I could eat a dozen."

"The bitter notes highlight its sweetness. It's smooth and rich and smells divine, and I'll take it."

Iris buys one of everything, naturally. And surprisingly, Alexia follows suit. Mitsugoshi arranges to have the items delivered straight to the castle. Even their service is exceptional.

"Alexia, shouldn't you ask them to gift wrap it?"

"No need."

"O-oh, okay."

Luna approaches the duo as they get ready to leave.

"Would you like to view some of our other products? I'm positive they'll tickle your fancy."

"Well…"

The girls didn't intend to stay long, but they're too curious to see other offerings from the company that developed chocolate—it's even enough to pique Alexia's interest.

"Yes, please."

"Wonderful."

With a quick word to her staff, Luna introduces one product after another—and not just candy. They have tea, liquor, accessories, daily goods, gourmet and preserved foods… All overflow with novel and fascinating qualities. The products basically force unexpected wads of cash out of their wallets.

And then a piece of cloth is set before them.

"What's this…?" Alexia tilts her head, pinching the lacy black material between two fingers.

"One of our panties for women," Luna introduces with a smile.

"Underwear."

"Really…?"

Iris and Alexia scrutinize the black T-shaped garment embroidered with white lace.

They can tell it's underwear when they look at it up close, but the size of the fabric seems way too small. Their butts would hang out if they wore these panties. Plus, some of the parts are see-through.

"We call them G-strings."

"G… G-strings?" Iris shudders and balks at the design that hides as little as possible.

While it's cute and all, its intentions are all too vulgar for Iris to stomach.

Sh-should these panties even be allowed to exist?

"As for gentlemen, they seem to like them very much."

Alexia's ears perk up.

"Iris…"

"Alexia, you can't be serious...?"

"I'm confident about the shape of my butt."

"Th-that's not the problem!!" Iris stammers.

What's this crazy kid saying?!

"P-p-p-p-please don't wear these! A princess should never don lewd clothing!"

"I'm confident about the shape of my butt."

"You've already said that! It's improper! Out of the question! I forbid it!"

"You can try it on, if you'd like."

Iris stops herself in the nick of time from snapping at Luna to mind her own business.

"Yes, please," replies Alexia.

"Don't do this!" Iris counters.

"Come on, Iris, I'm *just* trying it on."

"Yeah, right! I mean, you're basically setting up a situation where you *have* to purchase it! You're gonna act all indecisive, and then you'll just go and buy it anyway. I know how this works!"

Alexia irritably clicks her tongue in response.

"Your Highness, I hope there aren't any misunderstandings about our product. G-strings are made for women." Luna stands up. "In fact, I'm wearing that same model right now."

Luna turns her back to them, and the pair zero in on the shapely butt under her tight black dress.

"Look. Even though my dress is thin, you can't see my panty lines."

"Y-you're right."

Underwear lines are always visible under lightweight fabrics. There are girls who refuse to wear underwear to formal events to prevent them from showing.

But this G-string eliminates that problem. It can't be detected under clothing.

"Are you really wearing it...?"

"Would you like to see?" Luna asks, slowly peeling up her dress to reveal her milky thighs.

"I-I'm good!"

"Just kidding." Luna seductively grins and unfurls her dress. "Would you like to try it on, at least?"

"Yes."

"A-as long as you're just seeing how it looks..."

The duo trail after Luna into a large fitting room.

Iris nervously watches Alexia cheerfully slip out of one pair of underwear into another.

Alexia yanks her skirt up to her waist and pulls her white pair down, letting them fall to her ankles before lifting one foot and then the other. After hanging them on a hook on the wall of the fitting room, she spreads out the G-string in front of her.

"It's practically transparent...," notes Iris, sounding utterly baffled.

"Seems pretty airy to me," chirps Alexia, amused.

Alexia bends forward and raises her right foot, sliding the G-string up one leg and then the other. She tugs it up under her skirt and tilts her head curiously.

"It feels kinda weird...," Alexia comments.

Iris is at a loss for words when she sees her sister hiking her skirt up.

"That's..." Iris's vision goes completely white.

"Your Highness. You have it on backward."

"Oh, that explains it," Alexia replies to Luna, leaving her dumbfounded sister be as she slips off the G-string and puts it on the right way.

"Ooh, it feels nice."

"Yes, it's made from our new prized fabric."

Alexia kicks up, crouches down, and spreads her legs to test it out.

"Iris, look at this."

That pulls Iris back to reality.

"Look." Alexia jerks her skirt up to reveal a perfectly shaped butt that's almost completely exposed.

Her delicate white skin glows in the light of the fitting room. Alexia playfully shimmies her waist, and her buttocks jiggle around.

"S-stop that shameful behavior right now!"

"And see? No visible panty lines," adds Luna.

When Alexia lowers her skirt, Iris certainly can't see them.

"And check out the front. It's very cute."

Alexia hikes up her skirt again, turning to Iris. The design *is* cute, but it's…

"A-A-Alexia, it's completely sheer…"

"It hides enough."

Iris chants three times in her mind, *It's not enough, not enough, not enough.*

"I'll take three of these and all the other colorways."

"Thank you for your business."

"You can't! I absolutely forbid it!!" Iris snaps out of her trance. "Th-those undergarments are too perverse for the royal princesses of Midgar. I simply won't allow it!!"

"Iris…!"

"Neeeeeeeeeever, never, ever!!"

"But it's just a pair of panties!!"

The duo glare at each other. Luna can almost see the steam coming out of their ears.

"Fine."

"Alexia, you've come around."

"You know, I want to listen to you. I've always been swayed by meaningless words and lost sight of what matters. Like the time you told me you liked my swordplay."

With her see-through panties on full display, Alexia keeps her eyes warmly on Iris.

"Yeah, I remember that."

"My swordplay is a symbol of my small, insignificant life. That's why I want to listen to those who accept that about me."

"Alexia…" Iris is touched to the point of trembling. They're finally on the same page.

"If you can't accept G-strings, I won't buy them. I really, really, really want to wear them, but I won't if you don't want me to. So tell me: Are you absolutely sure G-strings are out of the question?" Alexia bores into her sister's eyes, as if peeking into her soul.

Iris wavers. "Um, I... Well, they're not totally unacceptable..."

"Not *totally* unacceptable?"

"...No."

"Then I'll take 'em!"

"Thank you for your purchase!"

Iris can tell she's been bamboozled, but she smiles and lets it go when she sees her sister beaming giddily.

The Eminence in Shadow

iestly can't remember what catalyzed this desire.

know is I've admired shadowbrokers for as long as

remember.

it a certain anime? Or was it a manga—or a movie?

guess it doesn't matter. I was all in for anything that featured a

ermind, or an eminence in shadow, as I like to call them. These

acters were never the protagonists or final bosses but were relegated to a role

nd the scenes where they flaunted their powers and meddled in the

rs of others. I've always looked up to the men in the shadows.

nted to be one of them.

All I know is I've admired shadowbrokers for as long as I can remember.

Was it a certain anime? Or was it a manga—or a movie?

Eh, I guess it doesn't matter. I was all in for anything that featured a mastermind, or an eminence in shadow, as I like to call them. These characters were never the protagonists or final bosses but were relegated to a role behind the scenes where they flaunted their powers and meddled in the affairs of others. I've always looked up to the men in the shadows. I wanted to be one of them.

Think of children who worship their favorite superheroes.

That was me but with master puppeteers.

Chapter 4

The Two Sides of the Shadow Garden?!

The Eminence in Shadow

Chapter 4

Summer's almost here.

I swing my wooden sword on a day in late spring. I'm in the middle of my practical elective. Now that I'm free from Alexia's clutches, I've transferred to be with Skel and Po. And because a bunch of students dropped out of the Royal Bushin elective after the Instructor Zenon scandal, all of us in section nine have been bumped up to section seven.

"Whatever happened with you and Princess Alexia?" Skel asks as he practices beside me.

"We haven't talked since the breakup."

Also, she tried to *kill* me.

"That's a shame. And you never even kissed?" prompts Po.

"No, never."

We're having a dumb conversation as we wave our swords around as usual. This is what life in section seven is all about. Even though it's a huge waste of time, this is the path I must take to maintain my status as a minor character.

"The Bushin Festival's coming up. Did you guys sign up for the qualifying round?"

"Of course! If I do well enough in the tournament, I can easily go home with two or three lovely ladies," boasts Skel. He's a virgin, by the way.

"Oh-ho-ho, with three, I'd have my hands full," comments Po, another big virgin.

"Cid, you didn't sign up for the qualifying round, right?"

The Bushin Festival is a massive, semiannual tournament. Besides the local fighters, famed knights from around the world come to participate.

There's a special bracket for students, and there are going to be preliminaries for our tournament. But an ordinary side character would never stand on a stage in front of everyone. Not in a million years.

"I'm not go—..."

"But don't worry! I went and signed you up! Show me your gratitu—... *Guhh!!*"

Skel suddenly clutches his stomach and crumples to the ground.

"H— Skel!! What's happened to you?" Po cries.

It's a frighteningly fast hit. I'm the only one who can see it.

"Hey. Hey, Skel. You should have seen yourself. It was like someone slammed you in the stomach with a right hook. What's up with you?" I ask as I loosen my right fist.

"Th-that's a really accurate description, Cid."

"This is bad. He's a goner. Gimme a hand to get him to the nurse's office. Hey, do you know if we're able to take back tournament applications?"

"Hmm, I'm not sure. Oh, Skel, you're foaming at the mouth."

Our instructor gives us permission to carry Skel to the nurse's office for his "sudden seizure" that knocked him out.

It's on the way there that I notice something.

"Who's that?" I ask about a solemn-looking group entering the school.

"It looks like...Princess Iris is with them."

Alexia is there, too. Our eyes meet for a moment before she scornfully turns away.

I still haven't told anyone she went all cuckoo on me and attempted to go on a wild killing spree. And I don't plan on telling anyone about the incident on the roof if she keeps her distance. With our peace treaty, she can kill whomever she pleases. Her swordplay seems to have really improved, and I think it's great that she's trying to get stronger. Well, as long as she doesn't try to kill me, that is.

"By the way, I heard Princess Iris is coming to campus to request some kind of investigation."

Po doesn't look it, but he's always in the know.

The Midgar Academy for Dark Knights is a massive building that contains the Midgar Academy of Science. I hear they conduct research and do science-y stuff. I dunno.

"I see."

Wait, didn't Alexia mention Iris is building a new army?

After Po and I watch the Knight Order enter the building, we drop Skel off in the nurse's office and just skip class.

There are a few people engaging in a discussion in a large reception room.

"We'd like to ask you, the most distinguished scholar in the kingdom, to interpret this artifact for us," continues a beauty with scarlet locks, Iris, holding a large pendant-shaped object.

"But I'm just a student," objects a lovely young girl with hair as pink as a peach upon taking one look at the artifact in question.

"Everyone in the world knows about your incredible work. You're Sherry Barnett, the best researcher in your field. No one could do it better than you."

"But..."

"It's a good opportunity for you. You should give it a try," interrupts a man in his early forties, encouraging Sherry.

"Assistant Principal Lutheran Barnett..."

"You can call me Father, you know," Lutheran nudges gently, chuckling.

In return, Sherry smiles awkwardly.

"Sherry, it's your time to go out into the world of professional research. Princess Iris's request will bring you closer to the bright future that's waiting for you."

"But I'm not..."

"Don't I say it all the time? Have confidence. I know you can do this. You're the only one who can." Lutheran places a hand on Sherry's slender shoulder.

"Fine, I'll do it…"

Iris hands Sherry the artifact.

"An ancient alphabet? It's written in a secret code," Sherry observes.

"There is a religious group that calls themselves the Cult of Diablos. This artifact was in their facility. They seem to be doing research on ancient civilizations, but we don't know the details. There must be a connection between the code and the ancient civilizations," explains Iris.

"Well, you certainly came to the right person." Sherry scrutinizes the object.

"I want a member of the Knight Order to guard it," Iris adds.

"What do you mean by guard…?" asks Lutheran.

"In all truth, the Cult of Diablos—that religious group—is after that artifact."

"That's unsettling." Lutheran sharpens his gaze.

"We originally obtained this from their facility. Of course, this isn't the only item we've confiscated. We've been storing other classified documents and objects in our warehouse, but I'm embarrassed to admit that an unidentified person burned down our warehouse the other day. This artifact is all that remains."

"Oh, I've heard about the recent fire. Which reminds me, Princess Iris, you established the new Knight Order after that."

"Yes, but it's still quite small."

"I believe it's called the Crimson Order, correct? I see you've brought your Crimson Knights here today."

"I have…"

"Are you that distrustful of the previous Order?"

Iris doesn't reply to Lutheran's razor-sharp question, looking back at him without changing her expression.

"Hmm. Fine by me. I'll approve up to two guards," concedes Lutheran.

"Two…? Well, I guess that won't be a problem if I'm guarding the artifact." Iris looks troubled.

"The work of the Knight Order will experience delays if Princess Iris is off-site."

The speaker is a broad-shouldered knight sitting to Iris's left. He's muscular with a beard as bushy as a lion's mane. A large scar runs across his cheek.

"Indeed… Glen, I leave the guarding to you."

"Understood, Your Highness," he says with a bow.

"Iris, I'll help, too," says Alexia from Iris's right. "If you split up the guards, fewer knights will be available to respond to the Ebony Incident."

Iris goes silent.

"The Crimson Order has its hands full, and I know who *he* is. I'm perfect for this role."

"But, Alexia, you're still…"

"A student. I'm a student, but age is irrelevant if you've got skill. You said it yourself."

"No, I didn't."

"That's what you've just told Miss Sherry." Alexia grins confidently at her peeved older sister.

"And you used to be so cute…," mumbles Iris.

"I heard that. Anyway, Iris, I want to know. I want to know why *they're* doing this and…if they plan to oppose us."

"But it's going to be dangerous."

"I know."

The sisters silently exchange glances.

"Fine. I formally request that you accept low-risk missions only and to the degree that it doesn't interfere with your schoolwork."

"Thank you." Alexia smiles and bows.

"I hope all goes well with the artifact," Iris addresses Sherry after letting out a deep sigh.

That evening, I try to cancel my application for the preliminaries after class.

"Thank you."

I bow and leave the student services office.

"Well, how'd it go?"

Skel and Po approach me outside the office. They were waiting for me.

"They said everyone's been paired up, and it's impossible to withdraw." I sigh.

"Hey, look on the bright side. If you do well, you're gonna be swimming in girls, right?"

"Yeah! They say tough times bring opportunity, if you know what I mean."

I shake my head. "I don't care if I win or lose. I just don't want to do it."

"Geez, you're hopeless. C'mon, I'm gonna introduce you to this special shop. Try to lose the long face."

"S-special shop?" stutters Po, taking ragged breaths through his nose.

"Oops, not that kind of special. I meant the Mitsugoshi that everyone's talking about. I've heard they've got all sorts of new items, and one of 'em is a snack called chocolate. It's supposedly sweet and hella delicious."

"Treats? I'd love some."

"You doofus! It's not for you." Skel slaps Po atop his head. "We're gonna give the chocolate to girls. Y'know, women go gaga for you if you give 'em something sweet!"

"O-oh, I get it. Spoken like a true professional, Skel. You always teach me so much."

"I know, right?" crows Skel, feeling full of himself.

"Come on, Cid. Let's get going."

"Let's go, Cid."

There's a sparkle in their eyes.

"Fine, I'll go," I agree with a sigh.

I have to admit I'm a bit curious to see what the chocolate of this world is like.

Skel takes us to the main street in the capital. The bustling evening streets are overflowing with people, and every store in this super-high-scale area seems packed to the brim. Mitsugoshi is more crowded than the rest of the shops by a long shot.

"Wow, it's so friggin' cool."

A brand-new, swanky building stands tall in the sky—trendy to the point that it seems almost contemporary. I haven't felt this out of my element since I walked into a high-end store in my past life.

There's an enormous line snaking out from the entrance. All the people waiting for their turn seem to be members of noble families or their guests. One glance is all I need to know these are wealthy, special customers. At the very end of the line is a woman in uniform holding a sign. The wait time is approximately eighty minutes.

"It's an eighty-minute wait," I protest.

"I'm sure we'll make it back before our dorm curfew," argues Po.

"We've already gotten this far. Let's go," insists Skel.

"But I've heard there are slashers on the loose. I don't want to stay out too late..."

"The three of us are friggin' dark knights, you nitwit. We'll slash 'em right back!" Skel pats the sword on his lower back.

"Y-you're right."

"Did you say slashers?" I ask, interrupting their conversation.

"I've heard there were recent killings in the capital, happening at night. And they've been carried out by expert fighters who've already taken down members of the Knight Order...," whispers Po.

"Ooh, creepy. I wouldn't be caught dead walking around at night."

A slashing cutscene? Sounds fun. Sign me up.

"Chop-chop! If we don't get in line, we won't make it in time for curfew," presses Skel.

Po and I trudge to the end of the line.

"Hi, m-m-ma'am. Y-you're pretty. G-g-got any hobbies?" Skel attempts to pick up the employee with the sign as soon as we get there.

But she flashes him a battle-hardened smile and proceeds to ignore him before staring at me with a cheerful grin for reasons unknown.

"Excuse me, sir. Could I have a moment of your time?"

She's an exquisite woman whose face is calm and refined with dark-brown hair that matches the color of her eyes. Her work uniform is a short and simple navy-blue dress marked with the Mitsugoshi logo. It reminds me of the flight attendants I saw in my past life.

"Who? Me?" I ask, pointing to myself.

"Yes. Please participate in our short survey."

A survey? That's a rarity in this world.

"Sure, I guess…"

"Thank you."

"I-I-I'll take the survey, too!"

"S-so will I!"

Skel and Po make a last-ditch effort to charm her.

"One customer will suffice," she replies, hooking her arm in mine.

Together, we cut the long line and make a beeline into the store. When I look behind me at the last second, I can see the disappointment in Skel's and Po's eyes.

I follow the woman into a boutique that seems excessively lavish. The interior isn't outwardly garish, but I can tell every last detail of decor has been carefully selected, and it gives off a chill vibe. Even the untrained eye can tell it's decorated in a modern and tasteful fashion.

She escorts me through the sales floor to a door labeled EMPLOYEES ONLY. I manage to sneak a few peeks around me, and every product that fills my vision is incredible.

Of course, I notice the rumored chocolate, but I also see coffee, makeup, and soap. It's the first time I've seen any of these in this world. Plus, their clothes, accessories, shoes, and underwear are all designed with class and novelty in mind. Even I know these items will fly off the shelves in this world. It's a no-brainer.

This place is unbelievable. It'll take the world by storm. It's only a matter of time, I'm certain.

We walk through the staff door and down a passage to a humongous stairway. I swear I've seen it in a certain movie about a luxury cruise ship. We ascend the stairs and continue walking through a bright and spacious hallway. At the very end of the hall is a large, sparkling door carved with exquisite engravings.

Two lovely ladies stand in front of the door. They bow to me and open it slowly.

What lies beyond is a space that looks like an enormous hall. There are tall pillars that resemble those in ancient Greek temples and marble floors that glisten under the light.

A red carpet has been unfurled, extending to the back of the room and flanked by two rows of attractive women.

"Huh?"

The moment I set foot in the room, they all kneel simultaneously.

"Um… So how about that survey…?"

An enormous chair has been positioned in the backmost part of the room. A crimson sunset pours down from the skylight and onto that delicate masterpiece.

The seat remains empty.

A lovely blue-haired elf stands next to it. She's a refined woman with a model-esque figure covered by an entrancing black dress. I know that face.

"We've waited a long time for you, my lord." Another woman stoops down to one knee with the elegance of an actress.

"Gamma…"

She's the third original member after Alpha and Beta. Anyone can tell she's a genius by taking one look at her clever face and sharp blue eyes. That's Gamma, the brains of the Shadow Garden.

Gamma is clever, I give her that. But she has one major flaw.

Her nickname is Gamma the Weak.

Even though she's one of the longest-serving members in the Seven Shadows, Gamma is the weakest by far. To backtrack, the Seven Shadows refers to the first seven members of the Shadow Garden. I chose that name because it's badass. Obviously.

When it comes to fighting and physical activities, Gamma's instincts are fatally poor. If Delta is the most talented fighter in the Seven Shadows, Gamma is the worst. I personally think the two of them are similar. If I

said that out loud, I bet Gamma would blow her fuse and Delta would tremble with mirth, but I know for a fact they're the same type of person.

I learned two things when I was teaching Gamma and Delta how to fight.

One: Intuition is wasted on an idiot.

Two: Intelligence means nothing without intuition.

At that point, I decided to try giving them the same instructions: *"Infuse your slash attack with a bunch of magic."* And that's all.

I was suggesting they physically pummel the shit out of their enemy—which is the brutish method I find absolutely abhorrent. That's right; my core beliefs crumbled before this duo without pomp or circumstance. If I even *think* about that day, I get a headache. Yeah, let's not go there. Forget about it.

"Nice to see you again, my lord." Gamma gracefully walks toward me like a model on a runway.

Her hips sway salaciously as I listen to the heart-stopping *tap, tap, tap* of her heels against the floor.

"ZOINKS!" She trips and falls over nothing.

"Th-these heels are too darn tall."

And she blames it on her shoes.

Gamma clutches her nose as she rises to her feet. Meanwhile, the women around her break into a lightning-fast whirlwind to produce shorter pumps.

"W-well, then. Come this way, Master," Gamma continues as if nothing happened, sauntering forward in totally different shoes.

But I don't really mind. There are only two ways to react when a girl embarrasses herself: either pretend not to notice or go all out and tease her. Even though I'm in the former camp myself, there's something I have to say.

"Your nose is bleeding."

The girls around her hastily wipe the blood away.

"R-right this way, my lord."

I glance at Gamma's burning-red cheeks. *She hasn't changed a bit.*

She escorts me to the giant chair, where I take a seat. The view is...fantastic.

Mighty fine, indeed.

There's a big and open space where a scarlet glow tumbles in through the skylight, and two rows of hotties are kneeling beside the red carpet. It's as if I've become king—the king of the Shadow Realm. Gamma must have spent a fortune preparing this set for me.

My heart is pumping. I'm moved to the core. I cross my legs, rest my cheek in my left hand, and raise the other, focusing my blue-violet magic into my palm and shooting it into the heavens.

It almost blasts into the ceiling before it dissolves into a myriad of lights that flood the entire room.

"Receive your reward…"

There is a downpour of light, falling upon the kneeling girls and temporarily dyeing their skin a bluish violet. It only replenishes energy, promotes magic circulation, and heals minor wounds… In other words, nothing much.

"I'll treasure this day forever." Gamma's voice wavers as she kneels at my side. Her performance is very convincing.

But she isn't the only one trembling. All the lovely ladies on both sides of the long red carpet are quivering, and some are even weeping. The employee who brought me here sniffles through her tears. Gamma is the perfect director for her troupe of actresses.

"You've done well, Gamma. By the way, I have a question about this company."

Yes, back to business. From the chocolate to the products on the sales floor to the architectural design of the building—I can't imagine them coming from this world.

"Ask me anything."

"Is this Mitsugoshi merchandise based off my stories?"

Gamma has always been interested in picking my brain for some reason. Every time Delta beat the living shit out of her, she would pester me in tears, begging me to tell her a story. That was when I told Gamma about my Shadow Wisdom, which included randomly embellished stories about chocolate and the other goodies in Japan from my past life.

"Yes, my lord. I've only re-created a fraction of the divine knowledge that you've imparted unto me."

"I s-see."

I only told her she could make chocolate by throwing together bitter beans and sugar and waiting till it hardens. Calling that knowledge is overkill. And how did she re-create all this? This must be what it means to have a brain. I mean, she's eons smarter than me.

But that doesn't bother me. The world has its fair share of geniuses and idiots. That's all there is to it.

But I do have one question.

"Do Alpha and the others know about this company?"

"Of course."

Oh, I get it.

They've fallen into their usual shindig of leaving me out. I understand if it's hard for them to include the only guy here in their clique of girls, but come on.

"A-and have you been making money?"

"Right now, we have shops in every major city both domestically and abroad. Our business is expanding at a rapid pace. But how long will we be able to hide in the shadows under the guise of a company? This is the most important consideration."

What's with the cheesy, slipshod setup? It's unnecessary. Just get to the point!

Basically, she's telling me that everyone is raking in dough from *my* knowledge. Everyone but me. If they just gave me a teeny-tiny portion of it, I wouldn't have scrounged for cash or chased down coins like a dang dog.

Whatever, it's fine. The girls have prepared this huge prop for me, so I can't complain.

But if I could just have a little slice of the pie.

"Um, I hope you don't mind me asking this, but could I borrow a few *zeni*?"

I'll pay her back someday…maybe.

"Yes, I'll prepare it right away," Gamma responds quickly.

She gives orders to the woman who brought me here.

A few moments later, a wheelbarrow full of coins rolls into the room, as tall as a mountain. I've never seen this many sparkling coins in one place. This is easily over a billion *zeni*.

"Th-this is a bit..."

I can't borrow all this. I could never pay them back.

"—gh! Is this not enough? I'll send for more right aw—..."

"No, it's fine." I stop Gamma midsentence and reach toward the coins, making a big show of thrusting my hand into the mountain.

The coins loudly clink together.

Now I've got their attention locked on my right hand. I concentrate with all my might.

"Hmph!"

I take about fifteen coins in my right hand and show it to everyone in the room, before slowly putting it into my right pocket. I've just gotten one and a half million *zeni* richer.

And I have another one and a half million *zeni* in my left pocket, too.

While focusing their attention on my right hand, I snatched some coins in my left at top speed, stuffing them into my pocket before anyone could notice. Alpha or Delta might have picked up on it, but Gamma never stood a chance.

"I-is that it? You can have all—..."

Watching her is hilarious to me. She thinks I'm only borrowing one and a half million *zeni*, but I actually pocketed three million!

"That's enough for now," I say, holding back laughter.

"All right. Take this back." Gamma claps, and the gaggle of women roll the wheelbarrow away.

Gamma kneels before me. "My lord, I think I know why you've come today. It must be about the incident."

"Yes."

I nod. *What incident?*

"My sincerest apologies. We're currently investigating the matter but haven't caught the culprit. Please be patient. I'll hunt down the slasher in the capital—the fools in ebony, pretending to be in the Shadow Garden."

"Hmm..."

This is the first I'm hearing about this.

"Hmm..."

Gamma gazes at Shadow as he trails off and begins contemplating. Somewhere in her blue eyes, there's a hint of unease.

A tear streams down from the corner of her eye without warning. Seeing those blue-violent rays reminds her of her past.

Gamma's life began with a light of the same hue.

If he'd never come, she would have died a rotting mound of flesh. She was abandoned by her family, chased out of her home country, stripped of everything in her possession. She fell into an abyss of pain and fear and disappointment—and the one who rescued her was the boy who produced the blue-violet light. She would likely never forget that glow for her entire life. To Gamma, it represents the light of survival.

Alpha once told Gamma there was life in it, and Gamma agreed, not for logical but for instinctual reasons.

It didn't just heal external wounds—but a much deeper part of the soul. When she touched the bluish light, it was as if she was released from her shackles, liberated from something holding her back. She finally felt like she had reclaimed her identity.

On that day, she was reborn. The moment she received the name Gamma, she vowed to devote her new life only to him.

While her intentions were sincere, she was the least powerful member of the Seven Shadows. She was defeated and surpassed by newer members, left crawling on the ground and deeply humiliated. Somewhere along the way, Gamma realized she couldn't beat her peers. It didn't matter how hard she trained.

She was in anguish. What was she worth? She would rather die than display her stupidity and bring everyone down. But he randomly called out to her the day she planned to end it all. And he imparted his Shadow Wisdom to her.

That insight showed her how to fight with her intelligence over strength, and she dived headlong into his ways. And since she thought this was her only chance at survival, she literally put her life on the line to re-create his Shadow Wisdom.

When Gamma looks back on it, she's certain he recognized her pain—that he shared his knowledge because he knew she was hurting and had foretold the path she would walk in life.

It made her feel forlorn. It saddened her to know he was out of her reach.

Does Shadow need me? Tears well up in her eyes whenever she thinks about it. But that's why she needs to wipe the tears away and keep fighting.

She'll make the Shadow Garden bigger and stronger, a more suitable organization for Shadow…and on that day, she believes her wish is certain to come true.

"I see. Very interesting." His voice pulls Gamma back to reality. "I think I know who did this. I'll take a look around."

Gamma's chest tightens when she hears his omniscient tone.

She'd failed to help him once again. He could surmise the correct answer with a snippet of information. Even if she mobilizes all her subordinates, he could easily find hints she never could.

But Gamma refuses to give up. One day, he's bound to notice her… so she has to persist.

"Nu, come forward." Gamma calls over the dark brunette who brought him here.

"This is Nu. She's number thirteen."

"Wow."

He peers at Nu through narrowed eyes. His gaze seems sharp enough to see to the depths of her power.

"Even though Nu only just joined us, even Lady Alpha has recognized her for her strength. Feel free to use her as a liaison, for chores or whatever you like."

"I'm Nu. It's a pleasure to meet you." Her voice trembles slightly from nerves.

"I'll call you if something comes up."

"Understood." She bows and steps back.

"I guess I'll be going now." He stands. "Oh, almost forgot. I'd like to buy some chocolate—the cheapest kind. If you could give me a friends and family discount, that'd be great."

"We prepare our best chocolate in-house."

"Um...how much will that be?"

"With the friends and family coupon, that'll be one hundred percent off."

"One hundred percent... That makes it free! Yippee, it's my lucky day! In that case, I'll take three of 'em."

"Thank you for your business."

Gamma smiles when she sees him return to the role of Cid Kagenou the normie.

"We're not gonna make curfew!"

"That's 'cause Cid took too long!"

"I said sorry and gave you chocolate."

The three of us sprint down the pitch-black streets of the capital.

I'm definitely one of the two reasons we're late. But Skel's and Po's constant questions about that lady are the other reason. Nu—was that her name? Either way, I just batted away their interrogation with a bunch of maybes.

That said, I never would have pinned Alexia as the type to become a real-life serial killer. If Delta's not the culprit, it's got to be Alexia. I knew it was her the moment I heard about the recent crimes. She's a princess who has it all. What could have possibly set her off...?

The woman's heart is an enigma.

You know, I don't look down on mass murderers. That's a way of life. But sullying the name of the Shadow Garden is a whole different story. Those unfortunate souls won't be getting away with this.

"Hey, did you hear that?"

"Nope, nothing."

Skel and Po are running ahead of me as they talk between themselves.

It doesn't seem they heard it well, but to me, it was crystal clear.

It was the sound of two blades colliding, which means people are fighting nearby.

I stop in my tracks.

"Yo, what's wrong?"

"We're gonna miss curfew!"

The duo pause shortly after I do.

I point to a back alley. "I'm gonna go take a shit."

They look like they can't believe I'm for real.

"If I don't go now, it's gonna stream down my legs when I run."

"That's an emergency."

"A question of curfew or pride."

Their faces turn serious.

"You guys go ahead. I don't want anyone to see me..."

"Ew... Gotcha! I won't tell anyone you took a dump outdoors!"

"No matter what anyone says...I think you made the right decision!"

"Oof, I can't hold it in. Hurry... Just leave me behind!"

"Cid... We'll never forget you!"

"Cid... Even if you poop outside, we'll always be friends!"

"Go! Gooooooooooooo!!"

The pair turn on their heels and book it out of there.

After I watch them skitter away, I head down the back alley, following the sounds of a duel. When I trace it to its source, I'm in the heart of the dark alley.

Two dark knights are in the midst of a fierce battle.

There's no doubt in my mind that the one in the school uniform and short skirt is Alexia. But the other is a masked man dressed entirely in black.

Something obviously isn't right. I could understand if Alexia wore jet-black, pretending to be in the Shadow Garden, but not the other way around. I climb to a rooftop and covertly watch them from above.

"Give it up already. There's no way you can win," says Alexia.

She seems to have the upper hand. The man in black isn't necessarily weak; he just can't touch Alexia, who greatly improved with her recent training.

His black coat is torn and tattered, and his blood is dyeing the cobblestones a dark crimson. One final push will determine the winner.

"Why do you kill the innocent? Is that why you fight?"

"We are the Shadow Garden..."

Just now, the man in jet-black definitely said, "Shadow Garden."

"Is that the only thing you can say? Is that what the man Shadow seeks?"

"We are the Shadow Garden..." The man in jet-black repeats himself.

Without a doubt, this man is the Shadow Garden impostor.

Sorry for doubting you, Alexia. It looks like you're innocent. My sincerest apologies.

But why is this guy impersonating the Shadow Garden?

That is the obvious next question, and I know the answer all too well. I can fully understand him, because I am who I am.

The answer is adoration.

This man is enamored by the Shadow Garden...and secret masterminds. I can't say I blame him. I mean, my whole journey began because I loved shadowbrokers. I fell in love with the hidden commanders in movies, anime, and manga and started imitating them.

This impostor walked that same path and found the Shadow Garden. Yes, he's the Shadow Garden's first follower in the world.

A warm feeling rises in my chest. I'm just happy to know a total stranger accepts us and our ways. I'm glad to know I've chosen the right path.

But this is unforgivable. Why? Because I'm a mastermind. If I forgive those who tarnish my organization's name, then I no longer am one. Right now, we can both call ourselves shadowbrokers, and I won't stand or settle for that.

"It's over for you."

When Alexia thwarts his counterattack by knocking the sword out of his hands, I feel another energy drawing near.

"It's over for you."

Alexia sends his sword flying, which clangs onto the cobblestone road.

"...Hngh!" Alexia tumbles, evading a sudden attack from behind.

She blocks another rapid strike, drives her foot into the assailant's stomach, and swiftly backs away. Glaring at her new opponents, she steadies her breath.

There are two more dark knights dressed in jet-black.

Alexia clicks her tongue as she watches the first man lift his sword.

This makes three, and she guesses they're all strong, too.

Against one of them? She could win easy. She has a good chance of taking two down. But to fight against three opponents is...

"It isn't very nice to pit three of you against a dainty girl."

I pray they humor her with an answer.

"How about three one-on-one battles? Or is that no good?" she suggests.

They're slowly surrounding her from all sides. She's making sure her back is covered as she inches away.

"Hey, look behind you. The moon is beautiful tonight."

One man nears her back, and she keeps him in check with her eyes. Their swords dart around with small movements as they attempt to gauge the other's intentions.

"Oh my. You're not going to look? I think you should." Alexia smiles. Her red eyes glisten in the moonlight.

"Because there's a lovely lady behind you."

"—gr...!"

She gets him.

Alexia moves instantly, swinging her bare blade down to slice her blockheaded opponent who turned back to check it out.

Die. She doesn't say it out loud but sneers at him instead. She rips through the black cloak, spraying fresh blood.

But the cut isn't deep enough. She just needs one more hit to finish him…

And in that moment, Alexia suffers a blow to the abdomen.

"Augh…!"

A black boot sinks into the side of her body, and she can hear her ribs snapping under impact. As she spits blood and slashes her weapon, she jams her sword into the black boot.

But the enemy evades her attack at the last second, and her blade bounces off the cobblestones.

The men are too far to attack.

Alexia hacks up blood and wipes her mouth. Her hand is stained red.

At this point, she successfully distracted two of them, but there is one left—the one who kicked her to stop her from killing the other man. Alexia glares at him spitefully.

Three against one. The numbers haven't changed.

But the situation has gotten worse. Two of them are unharmed, and the other is severely injured but capable of using his sword. She can't ignore the last man.

On the other hand, Alexia's lungs are punctured by her broken ribs. *They'll kill me*, she thinks. *I guess this is it.*

Alexia extracts a red pill from a pocket on her school uniform. She secretly nabbed the drug before the warehouse burned down. She's against brutish swordplay, but she prefers it to death. Alexia brings it to her lips. While praying that her impromptu strategy will work, she raises the pill to her lips.

At that moment, something inky comes down from the sky, landing as silently as an owl gliding through the night.

The black blade bisects one opponent, from which blood erupts. The suffocating stench of gore penetrates the alleyway. With a sharp swing, the man in ebony, Shadow, splatters the blood off his sword in a red line along the wall.

"To the fools who mock the name of the Shadow Garden…"

This is Shadow, the strongest being in existence. He's the one who demonstrates perfect swordplay—and the one she could never forget.

Is Shadow…fighting them?

That's what it looks like.

"Pay for your sins with your lives," Shadow continues.

In the next moment, the men in jet-black are set in motion, making an instant decision to spring from the cobblestones, bound off the wall, jump onto the rooftop, and flee.

"How pathetic..." Shadow moves to pursue them.

"Please wait...!"

Her voice stops him in his tracks. He turns back slowly, fixing his eyes on her.

Her sword trembles violently. She realizes...she is doing something stupid.

"I am Alexia Midgar, one of two princesses in this kingdom."

Shadow just stares at her. She knows he can take her life if he feels like it.

"State your purpose. What are you fighting for? Who are you fighting against? And...do you pose a threat to my country?"

Shadow turns his back to her.

"Stay out of it. Ignorance is bliss."

"Wha—...?! Wait, if you're saying you oppose the kingdom...!"

"And what would you do if I did?"

She's taken aback by his bloodlust.

Faced with an insurmountable force, she instinctively cowers. But defying our instincts is what makes us human.

"I'll fight you. I know you're going to try to kill my big sister, and I can't let that happen."

Shadow lets his coat billow behind him.

"I understand your swordplay. I may not be able to now, but someday, I'll..."

"Kill me?" he guesses.

With those parting words, Shadow vanishes into the darkness.

Alexia murmurs in the dark to herself. "Yeah, that's right..."

Silence returns to the night. Deserted and alone, Alexia clutches her stomach and huddles into herself. Her sword falls from her quivering hands. She knows she's done something stupid. But she's recently discovered a reason to fight: to protect the few things she holds dear—her only sister and her one friend.

"This isn't good…"

Alexia is about to pass out.

She knows something bad will happen to her if she blacks out in the alleyway. She tries using the wall to lift herself up.

"Alexia… Alexia!" A voice calls to her in the distance.

"Hey, Iris… Iris! Over here!"

"Alexia…!!"

The footsteps draw closer. Something soft catches Alexia in midair before her body hits the ground.

"Alexia! What have you done…?!"

"Iris…" Alexia buries her face in her sister's chest.

"Prepare yourself. I'll have you fill me in on all the details later."

"…Okay."

"Including this."

"Huh…?" Alexia sees the scattered red pills on the cobblestone road, where she dropped them. "Listen, Iris. I don't know anything about them."

"Quiet."

"I don't know. Honest."

"This is unforgivable."

"Oh, my head…" Alexia decides to let herself pass out and leave these things up in the air.

Two shadows dash through the dark streets of the capital.

As they grow concerned about attacks from behind, the men in black veer down an alley and skid to a halt. They appear to be in a hurry. They place their hands against the wall, trying to steady their ragged breath. For a few moments, only their harsh inhales echo through the dark alleyway.

Thunk.

A sound from the depths of the alley.

They quickly turn to peer into the darkness. A black silhouette takes form in the shadows, coming toward them.

Thunk, thunk.

The sound of his boots draws closer.

The men cautiously ready their swords. But then, a black blade is jabbed into one of their heads, instantly passing through the hapless soul's skull without warning.

"Agh… Aghh… Aghhh…!"

The ebony katana is withdrawn as the man shrieks in agony, spouting blood and dropping to the ground.

The remaining impostor starts backing away in fear when the figure emerges from the shadows and makes his appearance. In a black coat, he possesses a sword and keeps half his face hidden behind a magician's mask.

"Did I keep you waiting?" His voice is deep, as if resounding from the depths of the earth.

"Eek…!" yelps the man in black as he steps backward.

"Why are you afraid?" he asks. "Did you really think…you could escape?"

The man in black turns to flee.

"Wha—?!"

"Great work, Master Shadow."

He turns to find a woman standing there. She's alluring and elegant, wearing a short dress.

"You secured the culprit in no time at all. I'm in awe," she comments.

"Is that you, Nu?"

"Yes," she replies, continuing the conversation with the assassin sandwiched between them.

He backs up against a wall.

"Please leave the rest to me. I'll extract information from him."

The man in ebony lowers his sword.

"…Don't mess this up," he warns.

"Understood."

He turns on his heels and vanishes into the darkness. The lovely woman bows her head as she watches him depart.

The beauty and the man in jet-black are left in the narrow alley. The latter is fully armed, but the former is weaponless in a dress and heels.

The man acts quickly. With a series of rapid slashes, he stabs the unarmed girl to death.

At least…that's what he *hoped* to do.

With her dress upturned, she rends the night asunder with her white, sensual legs.

Ka-chank. The man's sword falls to the cobblestone road.

There's a beat before eight of his fingers drop next to it.

"A-aghh…!"

It's hard to tell if he's trying to retrieve his eight fingers or his sword. With only the thumbs remaining, he extends one of his hands.

But it's crushed by a high heel.

"Gyah…!"

With that, an ebony blade emerges from the toe of her stiletto. The blood from his fingers flows over the cobblestones.

"I'm not as kind as Master Shadow."

He can hear the bitterness in her voice. The man looks up to find a gaze cold enough to freeze him to death.

"Don't think I'll let you die in peace."

With the hem of her dress rippling through the air, she slams his chin with her milky knee.

The next morning, a ghastly corpse is found hanging over the main street in the capital. There is a message written in blood on its stomach:

THE PATH OF FOOLS

The face of the dead man is warped with agony and fear.

Lying in an immaculate bed, Alexia looks up to see her sister's stern face.

"I know what happened." Iris is seated next to the bed. "The murders weren't committed by the Shadow Garden but by impersonators from another organization."

"Shadow mentioned that," Alexia adds.

"Shadow, huh…? We still don't know what this organization is." Iris lowers her eyes in contemplation. "During the attacks on the capital, I identified the existence of a dark knight who may be in the Shadow Garden."

"The one who goes by Alpha."

Iris nods. "Other sources have indicated the Shadow Garden is an extraordinarily powerful organization. And your report confirms their name and the existence of a man called Shadow. But that's all we know. Everything else is a mystery. We don't even know their goal."

"Shadow was fighting the Cult of Diablos. Maybe their purpose has to do with them."

"Which makes the Cult our clue…" Iris lets out a sigh.

"Iris…?"

"I thought they were a normal religion that believes in Diablos the demon, but it looks like they're pulling the strings in more operations than we'd thought."

"Like that fire?"

"There's that. And the budget for the Crimson Order. I can't get the go-ahead, so I'll be funding it out of pocket for now."

Alexia knits her brows together. "Does that mean the Cult not only infiltrated the Knight Order but that they're also civil officers?"

"I don't know. They're either members of the Cult or taking bribes…but I can't say for sure. After all, I was reckless in throwing together the new Order."

"I'll help you pay for it."

"It's the thought that counts. You know how many members are in the Crimson Order, right?" Iris smiles bitterly.

"Eight."

"Right, just eight. With my contributions, they could easily survive for over ten years."

"Then can't we make the Order bigger?"

"It would be senseless to make it bigger now. We don't even know who we're fighting yet."

"Iris, um…" Alexia apprehensively looks up at her sister. "Which is the enemy of the Crimson Order: the Shadow Garden or the Cult of Diablos?"

Iris smiles. "Both. I refuse to allow any mischief in this kingdom."

"Iris… We shouldn't fight Shadow." Alexia clenches the bedsheets.

"Alexia, drop it…"

"Iris, you wouldn't say this if you knew him. I know you saw that attack that colored the night sky throughout the capital!"

"We've already concluded that was just the artifacts burning."

"But I saw him use his magic!"

Iris huddles close to Alexia and peers into her red eyes. "That sort of power is impossible for humans to achieve. Spending too much time in captivity has made your memory foggy. And I bet all those strange drugs made you hallucinate. I don't think you're lying, but I do think you need rest."

"Iris!"

Iris places both of her hands on top of Alexia's. "And even if it really did come from that Shadow, we can't turn a blind eye to him. Who will protect our country if I flee?"

"Iris…"

Iris strokes Alexia's hair, then rises to her feet. "Get some rest until you're healed."

"…I'll help you when I get better."

"That won't be necessary."

"Huh?"

"Oh, you're under house arrest. I must've forgotten to tell you."

"You can't be serious!"

"For stealing evidence." Iris shows her the red pills, and Alexia's jaw drops to the floor.

"Think about what you've done."

The door slams closed behind her.

The Eminence in Shadow

stly can't remember what catalyzed this desire.
now is I've admired shadowbrokers for as long as
remember.

a certain anime? Or was it a manga—or a movie?
guess it doesn't matter. I was all in for anything that featured a
rmind, or an eminence in shadow, as I like to call them. These
ters were never the protagonists or final bosses but were relegated to a role
d the scenes where they flaunted their powers and meddled in the
of others. I've always looked up to the men in the shadows.
ted to be one of them.

All I know is I've admired shadowbrokers for as long as I can remember.

Was it a certain anime? Or was it a manga—or a movie? Eh. I guess it doesn't matter. I was all in for anything that featured a mastermind, or an eminence in shadow, as I like to call them. These characters were never the protagonists or final bosses but were relegated to a role behind the scenes where they flaunted their powers and meddled in the affairs of others. I've always looked up to the men in the shadows. I wanted to be one of them.

Think of children who worship their favorite superheroes.

That was me but with master puppeteers.

Chapter 5

The Eminence in Shadow

Chapter 5

I'm being watched.

I feel their gazes when I walk into class. Everyone's watching me and whispering.

"That's him."

"The one who shit himself as he ran…"

"I heard he crapped on the street so everyone could see."

I shoot daggers at Skel and Po. Their eyes nervously flicker around the room.

"Th-that was a real disaster yesterday."

"G-good morning. It must've been tough for you."

"Yeah, morning. And today is much worse."

They wear a pair of stiff smiles, and I heave a huge sigh.

"A-anyway, did you bring your chocolate from yesterday?" Skel takes out a baggie.

"I brought mine," Po chimes in.

"Yeah, I guess," I say.

"All right. Come lunchtime, Operation: Give-a-Gift begins!"

"Ooh, I'm so excited!"

"Yeah, whatever you say."

Which brings us to lunch.

We follow Skel, who claims he'll show us how it's done.

He stands in the hallway near a classroom for the second-year students. We observe him from a distance.

"He's going for an upperclassman? Go, Skel."

"Yeah, whatever you say."

After a few seconds pass, a cute girl exits the classroom.

"Uh, um…here." Skel holds out the chocolate.

"Hey, you got some business with my fiancée?" A pair of large hands clutch his shoulders.

There's a crazy-buff senior behind him.

"Oh…I…I just…"

"Let's take this outside. Y'know, to talk it out."

The two of us ignore his distressed stare and turn away.

"Let's go."

"Yeah, whatever you say."

I can hear Skel screaming behind me.

Po takes me to the library. It's an enormous resource shared between the academies for dark knights and sciences. Naturally, this isn't where the jocks of the school hang out. Though, of course, it's not for me, either.

"Which means you're after someone from the Academy of Science."

"Yes. I'm not taking Skel's approach. See, I did a thorough investigation on her. I know her friends; her favorite foods; her dorm room number; which bathroom she uses; her shoe size and the smell of her feet; the color of her underwear; her hip, bust, and waist measurements; and I used a cup she drank from to…"

"All right, enough. Just go already."

I drag Po into the library and walk away. I don't see what happens next.

"Eeeeeeeeek!! It's that guy! My stalker!"

Almost instantly, I hear screaming behind me.

The bag of chocolate sways as I walk around the library. I usually never come here. It's nice.

I speak to the first girl from the Academy of Science that I pass. "Here's some chocolate."

"Huh?" She's a hottie with light-pink hair.

I hand off the bag of chocolate and leave.

"Wait! What?"

I can hear her getting all confused. I think I've seen her face before, but I can't remember where.

"I wonder what this is."

A cute girl with peach-colored hair in the study room cocks her head to the side. She scrutinizes the brown objects in the box with relaxed eyes. Even after taking the fragrant thing in her hand, she can't identify it. She's almost certain the boy had called it chocolate when he gave it to her.

"Sherry, are you all right?"

There's a middle-aged man standing behind her with salt-and-pepper hair all slicked back.

"Assistant Principal Lutheran..."

"You promised to call me Father in private."

"Foster Father." Sherry smiles uncomfortably.

"Why do you have that box of chocolate?"

"Chocolate? A boy from the Academy for Dark Knights gave it to me."

"You don't say." Lutheran thoughtfully strokes his beard. "That's the luxury snack. All the girls have been talking about it. I think he gave it to you as a gift."

"What? But I don't even know him."

"They call it 'love at first sight.' That's the finest chocolate in the world. You can line up for it at the crack of dawn and still not be able to purchase it. He must have done the impossible to get it for you."

"Love at first sight...," Sherry murmurs, her cheeks tinged pink.

"How will you answer him?"

"Answer him...?"

"He must be waiting for your response."

"B-but I..." Her face flushes bright red, and her eyes dart back and forth.

"You're not just here to do research. You should learn how to interact with your peers. That's what school is for."

"...I will."

He gently grins at Sherry, who's hung her head.

"Is all going well with the artifact?"

"I've only just started." Sherry smiles uneasily, her cheeks still slightly flushed.

"That's totally understandable."

"But I do know one thing: It's written in a unique code."

"A unique code?"

Sherry spreads documents across a table. "I'm guessing it was used by an ancient country or organization. And...it's almost identical to the one from Mother's research."

"Oh, Lukreia's... She was a great researcher, too." Lutheran closes his eyes as if remembering the past.

"I need to crack the code that Mother researched right before she died."

The face examining the documents was that of a brilliant researcher, no question.

"It's just the right job for you."

"Thank you."

When Lutheran lightly pats her head, Sherry is bashful.

"Where is the artifact now?" he asks.

"A knight is guarding it in the other room."

"You're not holding on to it?"

"Only if it's necessary. It's important for me to think in peace. Plus, I get too nervous around the knights."

"I see. *Cough, cough...* E-excuse me..." Lutheran turns away to hack.

"Foster Father! Are you all right?" Sherry panics and rubs the back of a skeletal man with sunken-in cheeks.

"I-I'm fine. It's okay." Lutheran calms his breath. "And I was just feeling good the other day. I guess illness can be unpredictable."

"Foster Father..."

"Don't worry about me. More importantly, I received another message from the college town asking if you'd like to study abroad."

"The college town, Laugus..."

"The most brilliant scholar in the world has acknowledged your research. If you study in Laugus, your skills will only improve. It's a fantastic offer."

Sherry shakes her head. "I can't leave you alone sick, Foster Father."

"You don't have to worry about me, Sherry."

"I would have died if you hadn't taken me in when Mother passed away. I'm going to help you...for helping me," she states with tears forming in her eyes.

"Sherry...you're a wonderful daughter," Lutheran replies with a kind smile. "Good luck on your research. And eat your chocolate."

"...I will."

Lutheran exits the study room. Sherry puts the chocolate in her mouth.

"It's sweet... It's delicious."

She reaches for a second piece.

I'm on my way back home after an Alexia-less, Skel-less, Po-less day.

The campus has assumed the orange hue of the setting sun. I walk through the campus, where there aren't many students, when a girl suddenly approaches me. Her uniform indicates she's in her second year at the Academy of Science. Her dark-brown hair is pulled back into bun. A drab pair of glasses covers her dark-brown eyes.

But a seasoned extra can tell: She's an inconspicuous beauty who's pretending to be a minor character.

"Hey, can I talk to you for a minute?"

I've heard that voice before.

"Nu?" I whisper. She nods in reply.

It's crazy how a change of hair and makeup can conceal an elegant woman.

"Are you planning on going to school here?" I ask in a hushed voice.

"No, I'm just borrowing the uniform. It helps me blend in with the others."

"I see."

I don't know most of the students here. As long as she's in uniform, there's a good chance she'll stay undetected.

"Where do you want to talk?"

"Let's head to that bench."

There's no one near the seats that overlook the campus, and the two of us sit under the dazzling glow of the sunset.

Nu surveys the academy. Behind her glasses, she narrows her eyes.

If her life had gone differently, she would have been in her second year. Until the day she was abandoned for being possessed, she always believed she would have a peaceful, successful future.

But that ended up being nothing more than a fantasy.

For little did she know, everything she took for granted—her friends, family, life itself—rested atop a thin tower of ice. Nu was a happy child who didn't know what lurked underneath that fragile construct.

Her eyes observe the students in envy and sorrow, and she recognizes a few of their faces.

In many social circles, Nu was known as the daughter of the marquess, living an affluent lifestyle.

But that time in her life has passed. She's been erased from the history of her household, as if she never existed.

She wonders how many of her friends still remember her.

Maybe they talk about her. But she guesses they'd rather spread hateful rumors.

That's what happens to the possessed.

There's no reason she has to meet Shadow at school in daylight, but she can't relinquish her last shred of hope. She wants to believe she has a place in a tranquil corner on this campus. She wants to relish in this foolish dream.

Nu smirks.

She has no place to call home, but she has comrades who share the same goal. And sitting right next to her…is her beloved master.

He started fighting all by himself. Even if he was the last man in the world, he would continue to fight. His existence is what keeps the Shadow Garden afloat.

People are frail and want to rely on something definite. If god is essential to Earth, then Shadow is essential to the Shadow Garden.

But she believes he's better than god. If she opens her eyes, she can see him—and if she reaches out, she can touch him.

"Hmm? What's up?"

"There's something on you." Nu wipes a stray thread off his shoulder and looks at his profile. "Please don't tell Gamma about this. She'd be so mad if she found out I snuck onto campus in broad daylight."

"You got it. But I was really surprised. That makeup makes you look totally different."

"My face is bland, so it's easy for me to change my appearance. I've always been good with makeup. I guess you could call it one of my old hobbies."

"Wow, and your Mitsugoshi persona?"

"When I'm there, I make myself look much older than I really am."

"I see. By the way, how old *are* you?"

"It's a secret." Nu flashes a beguiling smile. "I'm here to report on the incident yesterday with the man in black."

"Great."

"I interrogated the pretender but couldn't get anything out of him. I suspect rigorous brainwashing destroyed his psyche. Judging from his other physical characteristics, I believe he is a Third Child."

"Huh?"

The Children of Diablos.

If the Cult finds impoverished orphans or young citizens who possess even the slightest bit of magic, its members will snatch them from the streets and raise them in a special facility. There, the children undergo brutal training and brainwashing. They're loaded with drugs, and it's said that fewer than 10 percent of them manage to "graduate."

The Third Children are those in the 10 percent who are deemed worthless. They only exist to be sacrificed and abandoned. With minds too corrupted to leak classified information, the Thirds are more powerful than the average knight.

The Seconds are mentally stable. The few Firsts in existence are said to be the greatest warriors in the world.

Nu doesn't tell Shadow that, of course. She doesn't think she has to explain common knowledge to him.

"The Cult is clearly pulling the strings in these incidents. I imagine their purpose is to lure us in."

"Hmm."

"But that isn't their only goal. The other day, we confirmed the existence of a Named First Child in the capital. He's called Rex, the Game of Betrayal. I'm guessing they're gathering for a particular purpose. Right now, we're not sure where Rex is, but we're currently investigating the matter."

"Hmm?"

The Named Children.

They are the Children of Diablos who have made extraordinary contributions to the Cult. Most of the Named are First Children, but there are rare cases of a Second. There are Named who have risen through the ranks to the Knights of Rounds, which is why it's said this title is the gateway to success.

And one member of the Shadow Garden used to be a Named First Child. All this information has been provided by that same woman.

But Nu skips over these details, of course. She figures he already knows this.

"Please be careful. The Cult is up to something. We'll keep investigating and report back as soon as we know more."

"Hmm."

The evening sun is sinking beneath the horizon. This dim glow of the sun turns the clouds vermilion.

Nu fans her neck, which is slightly sweaty from the heat, and stands up. After stretching beside her, Shadow rises to his feet.

There could have been a future where they spoke as lovers and spent their days together at school. Nu smiles wistfully, imagining what might have been.

And even if it's a moment of indulgence…

"Hey, don't you know how to escort a lady?"

"Escort? You mean like this?"

He sticks out his left arm, and she links with him, walking side by side, and smiles.

This was the future she should have had.

A male student screams from far away. "Shit spillerrr!!"

Nu crossly clicks her tongue.

She recognizes the boy who ruin the mood. He's the piece of trash who would constantly hit on her in social circles. She decides to beat him up afterward.

Next to her, Shadow looks around nervously for some reason. Nu squeezes his left arm.

Who's the strongest dark knight in school? Two years ago, the answer would have been Iris Midgar.

After she graduated, there would come a time when no champion reigned over the Midgar Academy for Dark Knights. At least, that was what everyone thought.

But a champion appeared out of the blue.

An unexpected person assuming an unusual form rose to absolute dictatorship over the academy.

And her name is Rose Oriana.

She's a transfer student from the land of art and culture, known as the Oriana Kingdom, where she is daughter of its ruler, King Raphael Oriana.

The Oriana Kingdom and the Midgar Kingdom are allies. And although she was expected to transfer to the Midgar Academy for Dark Knights, no one ever imagined she'd become the unrivaled champion at school.

Frankly, it doesn't matter whether it was expected.

The problem is Rose Oriana is my opponent in the first round of the preliminary tournament.

I do have the option to withdraw.

Skel got tough love from an upperclassman in a body slam. Po got disciplinary action for sneaking into the girls' dormitory. Which basically means I can get out of the preliminaries if I make up an excuse.

But now that I think about it, losing to the undefeated champion in the first round is exceedingly normcore.

It's fitting for a minor character—there's no mistaking it.

I won't be withdrawing. My mission is to partake in the most normie fight in the world—for normies, by normies!

Which is why I'm now drawing my sword in front of a huge audience.

Princess Rose Oriana is standing right before my eyes.

With her honey-colored locks elegantly curled, Rose dons stylish fighting gear and wields a slender sword. The curves in her face are gentle, her figure is stellar, and everything about her is just plain chic. It's what one could expect from the princess of the country of the arts.

To top it off, Rose is also Student Council president despite being a transfer student in her second year. Thanks to her beauty, strength, and popularity, people are cheering enough to rock the stadium.

No one is shouting my name. I sort of wish they would cheer for a fellow countryman, but whatever.

This is the stage for a side character. The best one of all.

My sword violently shakes in my hands.

I wonder if I've ever felt this nervous before a fight. She could claim victory, commit murder, vaporize me without a trace, but that's all too simple. No one wants to see a cop-out. They want to see me lose harder than anyone else.

How does one define *normie-ness*?

I'm stepping into philosophical territory here.

But have no fear. I've mastered the Forty-Eight Hands of Minor Mystery technique in preparation for this day.

"Rose Oriana versus Cid Kagenou!" the judge announces.

Electric sparks shoot from our eyes—her honey-colored irises and my normie ones.

Hey, Rose Oriana. Can you keep up?

Keep up in the ultimate fight with a background character!

"Let the battle begin!!"

Rose's rapier begins dancing through the air the moment the match starts. It draws beautiful, sharp spirals as it approaches my chest.

If I was a real side character, I wouldn't be able to react in time.

But I can see it.

I see it…and I don't flinch. I can't let her see a single reaction.

Why? 'Cause that's how we roll.

I won't move an inch until the rapier hits my chest. The tip of the weapon is blunt for this preliminary round, but that doesn't mean I'll come out unscathed.

The rapier touches my chest.

At that moment, I make my move.

Without showing any other movements, I lunge back using the strength in my toes, and I use the force of the rapier pushing against my chest to add a spin.

From a secret pocket near my wrist, I tear open a bag filled with blood that I collected for this day.

All this has taken less than ten deciseconds.

I'm spinning backward as I spout blood like a fountain.

"PLEEEEEEEEEEEEEGH!!"

As a ruby tornado, I create a beautiful masterpiece of splattered blood.

I call this my Hidden Normie Technique: Spinning Guard, Bloody Tornado.

I clumsily bounce off the floor and roll over.

The cheers from the audience shake the arena.

"Guh…guh…gyaaaaaahhhhhh!" I slice open another bag and start spewing blood everywhere.

It's perfect!

Everyone in this venue totally buys that I'm a side character. I almost flash my pearly whites after my perfect-ten performance, but I stop myself.

It isn't over yet.

That's right. This isn't the end.

"Gurg, ga-aaah, AAAAAARGH!!" I rise to my feet, pretending I'm literally ten seconds away from death.

Yeah...that's because there are still forty-seven techniques left.

How is he standing?

Rose Oriana is stunned by the boy who keeps getting back up no matter how many times she knocks him down.

He's soaked in blood, and no one can tell if he can lift up his sword. He doesn't look like he can fight— No, it's a miracle he can even stand.

Although her sword is thin, her attack certainly isn't light. The tip of her blade may be blunt, but the magic inside of it is real. If she got one decent shot, he'd be rendered useless.

But...exactly how many times has she hit him?

It wasn't just once or twice. Even though he endured at least ten strikes, he still rises to his feet with unrelenting vigor.

How is he still standing after all that? His body has exceeded its physical limits, but his eyes seem devoid of death.

His fierce gaze tells her he still has something left to do.

That's right. His soul surpasses the limitations of the body, and his unyielding soul is holding his broken being together.

His valor leaves a deep impression on Rose. How badly does he want to win this battle and why? He must have a reason he can't allow himself to lose.

There is an immense difference in skill. He doesn't have so much as a one-in-a-million chance, but even then, he refuses to give up.

His fiery eyes glare at Rose.

It isn't over yet. This isn't the end.

Rose is moved that the tenacious spirit of a hero can defy death in the face of an undefeatable opponent. She has great respect for him, offering her deepest apologies for assuming it'd be an easy victory. He's certainly hopeless when it comes to a sword fight, but as for the battle of spirits, Rose has completely lost.

"You'll perish with my next attack."

Which is why she chooses to end it quickly. If he keeps this up, he'll get up until he dies. That and…she didn't want to kill a promising young fighter.

No one is cheering in the arena anymore. Everyone watches the boy in horror.

Her sword reaches the apex of magic on this day. The sky quakes, and the people in the audience, concerned, mumble to one another.

"Looks like you're not giving up."

His eyes burn brighter and brighter, not even slightly fearful of her oncoming attack but instead displaying an insatiable determination to fight.

He leaves her with no choice but to unleash her full power.

Rose's sword hums through the air.

"Stop!! That's enough. This battle is over!"

The referee steps between them and ends the match. He judges it would be too dangerous to continue.

Rose is relieved, simply put.

But the boy feels differently.

"Come on! I've still got thirty-three left…"

His eyes are screaming, *I can still fight!*

"The winner is Rose Oriana!!"

A mighty applause congratulates Rose.

She waves back at the audience before bowing deeply to Cid, who's in a heap on the floor.

I was almost brought to the first aid office after preliminaries, but I slip away when no one's looking.

That was a close one.

If anyone saw I was unscathed, it'd be a huge mess. Had I stayed any longer, I might've had to start taking swings at myself.

I leave through the player entrance and walk down an empty hallway.

I guess I'll have to wait until next year to show off the rest of the thirty-three esoteric techniques. Or I bet I'll have a good opportunity to use them before then.

"U-umm..."

"Hmm?"

An unfamiliar student calls over to me out of the blue. I don't recognize her voice. I'm not sure, but I feel like I've seen this peach-haired cutie in her uniform for the Academy of Science before.

"Are you hurt?"

"I've just barely avoided...anything serious...maybe?" I casually pose with my hand to the wound on my chest.

"I'm glad to hear that. I watched your fight."

"O-oh, really."

"I don't usually watch battles, but I thought it was really cool the way you stood up over and over again."

"Er, 'cool'...?"

"Yeah..." Her cheeks turn pink, and she nods.

To think a normie is cool. Geez, she has weird taste. I guess there were a lot of spectators, so it isn't too odd there were oddballs in the bunch.

"Um, here..." She timidly holds out a small pouch.

"What's this?"

"I baked you cookies. In return for the..."

It must be a thank-you for putting on a good show.

"Thanks."

I figure *Why not?* and take them.

She smiles cheerfully.

"I-if you wouldn't mind, I'd like to start off as friends."

"Friends? Sure thing."

My general policy is to not embarrass women—with a few exceptions.

"Yay! Foster Father, I've made a friend!"

Foster father?

I follow her line of sight to see a middle-aged man walking toward us. He has black, slicked-back hair with gray streaks. I know I've seen this skeletal fellow before.

"Assistant Principal Lutheran..."

I've heard the assistant principal of this school is a master swordsman who's won the Bushin Festival.

Which means this girl who loves him as her foster father must be...

"Sherry Barnett...!"

"Yes?"

According to my personal research, she has the most potential to become the main character in the Academy of Science. I believe she's supposed to be in a position where she gives the protagonist advice, solves the greatest mysteries, and creates powerful, Boss-toppling devices. I never thought I would have to fight someone from the Academy of Science, so I honestly didn't care and forgot all about her.

"You must be Cid Kagenou." Assistant Principal Lutheran stands next to Sherry.

"Yes."

"Any injuries?"

"I—I was miraculously... Oh yeah. Maybe she went easy on me?"

The assistant principal strokes his chin, quietly confirming my suspicion.

"Yes, I think Rose was holding back. But you must get yourself to a doctor."

"Yes, absolutely."

I absolutely *won't* be doing that.

Lutheran nods and places a hand on Sherry's shoulder.

"This girl always has her nose in her research, so she doesn't have many friends."

"Foster Father!"

The assistant principal merrily chuckles and continues to speak. "I wasn't always able to laugh like this, you know. Sherry and I have been through a lot. I hope you two can get along. It's all a father could wish for."

Lutheran's face is stern as Sherry stands beside him with an uncomfortable smile.

I only befriend side characters…but there's no way I can say that.

"…Sounds great."

"Well, I'll leave the rest up to you youngsters." The assistant principal pats my shoulder and leaves.

"Um, it's nice to officially meet you."

"Nice to meet you, too."

"So what do you want to do?" She tilts her head. "Oh, right. We have to get you to a doctor before anything else. I'm sorry for getting carried away."

She smiles uneasily.

"No, don't worry about me. I'm fine."

"That may be true, but…"

"I don't need to see a doctor. I'll go later. Seriously, I will. Okay? Yeah, so let's go out for tea or something."

"Um, are you sure you're okay?"

"Positive."

"Dark knights are incredible."

"Yep."

This stunner flashes me a smile. She's the furthest thing imaginable from a background character.

After that, the two of us eat her cookies and talk over tea. We go our separate ways when we finish. Though a perfectly average girl in conversation, she seems to be flooded with requests from the Knight Order, currently conducting research on a sacred artifact. I went the extra mile and told her I was impressed. Oh, by the way, her cookies were simple but downright delicious. She can never be a normie's friend.

But she goes to the Academy of Science, so we probably won't meet again anyway.

The next day, I notify the school that I'll be taking five days off for medical treatment to ease their suspicions.

My classmates are a little nicer to me when I finally come back.

Ever since Sherry befriended Cid, she feels like she's floating on air.

Cid has been absent from school due to the injuries he sustained at the preliminaries.

He said he felt fine after the tournament and even joined her for tea, but he seems to have overdone it after all. She's worried about his condition.

She thinks about visiting him but doesn't want to be a bother. But something is gnawing at her, and she needs to talk.

"Whew…" Sherry stops analyzing the artifact and lets out a sigh.

She can't focus on her work. Her head is too far in the clouds.

The afternoon sunlight flows into the study room.

No matter what she does, he's all she can think about.

She thinks back to the moment he gave her the chocolate, about his unrelenting stance during preliminaries, about their conversation over tea—over and over again.

She thinks about him during class and as she conducts her research, right until she goes to bed.

"I wonder what's wrong with me…?"

She retrieves the empty box of chocolate from a drawer in her desk.

Even though she had already eaten the contents, she could not find it in herself to throw away the beautifully decorated box.

The sweet aroma of chocolate still clings to it.

Sherry is also curious about a certain rumor.

From what she's heard, Cid and Princess Alexia are in love.

She doesn't know the specifics, but she imagines the rumor holds up for it to make its way from the Academy for Dark Knights to the Academy of Science.

"Mm!" Sherry stretches as she watches the curtain billow with the wind.

"Okay. I'll do it."

She can't concentrate on anything.

Sherry decides she has to talk it out in person.

Knock, knock.

Sherry gives a few quick raps on a door in the dormitory for girls. That's where the student in question is supposedly under house arrest.

"It's me, Sherry Barnett, the second-year student at the Academy of Science." She introduces herself through the door and waits for a response.

"Hello," replies a voice at the same time the door swings open. "Is there anything I can do for you, Sherry?"

"Yes. Apologies for the sudden visit."

"Come on in," suggests the room's resident, Alexia.

Her place is spacious and serene, much larger than the average dorm lodgings. Sherry is told to make herself at home and perches on the couch.

"Would you like black tea? I've also got coffee. Seems to be really popular recently."

"Oh, I don't need anything."

"It's no trouble."

"O-okay. I'll take a coffee."

"All right." Alexia begins gracefully brewing a pot.

Sherry starts getting nervous. *I'm in my second year, and she's only in her first. No need to get worked up*, she reassures herself with nonsensical logic, thinking it's all good because she's Alexia's senior. But on second thought, Alexia *is* royalty.

Maybe this isn't such a good idea.

No, no—she's the upperclassman here. She has to be confident.

"I can guess why you're here, Sherry."

Sherry jolts at those words. "U-umm…"

"This is about the artifact, right?"

"Well, not exactly."

There's the *clink* of a coffee cup. Alexia places it on the table in the midst of an awkward lull in the conversation.

"Here you go."

"Th-thank you very much."

Alexia takes a seat opposite Sherry.

"Whoa, that's bitter…," Sherry whispers after taking a sip.

"It's easier to drink if you add milk and sugar."

"O-okay."

Sherry didn't mean for Alexia to hear that comment, but it looks like she did. Sherry's automatic reflex is to add tons of milk and sugar and chug it.

"Oh, it's so good."

"G-great… Those are the finest coffee beans from Mitsugoshi. I'm glad you like it."

"Mitsugoshi… Oh, the place that sells chocolate. You know, that place really is something. This coffee is so sweet and creamy."

"Uh, yeah, it sure is…," Alexia comments, looking as if she wants to say, *Because you're basically drinking sugar and milk.*

"So what can I do for you?"

"Oh, right. Yes." Sherry puts down her cup, looking slightly pained as she mumbles, "Actually, I'd like to ask you something."

"Okay."

"Um, like…if you've had a boyfriend recently and stuff."

"I'm sorry…?"

"A-and if you went out with Cid Kagenou and whether you're still together and stuff."

"U-um…" Alexia scrutinizes her face to find out if she's being serious.

Sherry's eyes are darting around the room, and there's obvious tension in her shoulders.

Alexia guesses she may not be good at conversation in general. She's picked up that Sherry is nervous, but Alexia can't figure out the reason behind her question.

"We broke up." Alexia speaks as calmly as possible.

"Really? Phew..." Sherry sounds elated, as if she feels relieved from the bottom of her heart.

Alexia's cup clinks as she sets it down.

"Oh, but...but does that mean you actually dated...?" Her tone changes drastically and sounds uneasy.

"It wasn't a real relationship. There were some circumstances that required us to pretend."

"Oh, I see. That's great." Sherry giggles cheerfully.

Alexia's cup clangs.

"I just befriended Cid the other day."

"What? Y-you don't say..."

"Yes. I couldn't stop thinking about your relationship."

"Um, was that the only reason for your visit?"

"Yep! It distracted me so much, I couldn't focus on my research. I'm just so happy to know you two aren't dating!"

"Y-yeah, great."

Alexia brings the cup to her mouth with a trembling hand. It's empty.

"Thank you so much! Oh, and thanks for the coffee!" Sherry takes her leave with a bright smile—the exact opposite of the expression she wore when she came in.

The moment she steps out of the room, there's a sound of something breaking, but Sherry is too ecstatic to hear it.

The Eminence in Shadow

nestly can't remember what catalyzed this desire.

l know is I've admired shadowbrokers for as long as

n remember.

s it a certain anime? Or was it a manga—or a movie?

I guess it doesn't matter. I was all in for anything that featured a

stermind, or an eminence in shadow, as I like to call them. These

racters were never the protagonists or final bosses but were relegated to a role

ind the scenes where they flaunted their powers and meddled in the

irs of others. I've always looked up to the men in the shadows.

anted to be one of them.

All I know is I've admired shadowbrokers for as long as

I can remember.

Was it a certain anime? Or was it a manga—or a movie?

Eh. I guess it doesn't matter. I was all in for anything that featured a

mastermind, or an eminence in shadow, as I like to call them. These

characters were never the protagonists or final bosses but were relegated to a role

behind the scenes where they flaunted their powers and meddled in the

affairs of others. I've always looked up to the men in the shadows.

I wanted to be one of them.

Think of children who worship their favorite superheroes.

That was me but with master puppeteers.

That Scene Where Terrorists Take Over the School

Chapter 6

The Eminence in Shadow

Chapter 6

The day after I return to school, my last class of the afternoon ends a bit early.

"The candidates for Student Council and our current student president will now give speeches. Everyone, please return to your seats." The instructor addresses the students trying to book it out of class.

"Where are the third-year students anyway?"

"Who knows."

I answer Skel's random question with a yawn. He's sitting next to me.

"The third-years are out the whole week for an after-school program…"

Right when Po turns back in his seat to inform us, the door swings open. Two girls enter as the instructor leaves the room. I know one of their faces. She was my opponent from the other day: Rose Oriana, the Student Council president. I've always wondered how a normal school uniform can exude chicness when someone trendy is wearing it.

"Um, today, our instructor has given us this precious time to tell you about the Student Council election…," starts a girl in her first year stiffly, as if she isn't used to public speaking.

Am I the only one who feels like this speech is going in one ear and out the other?

Skel and I yawn as we space out through the speech. Po seems to be taking notes.

Wait, I'm pretty sure I just made eye contact with the student president. I would be surprised if she remembered the insignificant background character she squashed in the first round.

"Hey, the student president just looked at me," says Skel, fixing his bangs.

"Yup," I respond.

"Hey, hey. She might scout me for Student Council."

"Yup."

"Hey, hey, hey. Being on the council would bug me. I'd hate it."

"Yup."

This is how we pass the time. Then, out of nowhere, my magic feels off.

"Huh?

"What is this?"

I'm constantly training by manipulating magic particles in my body, but now it feels like I can't contain them anymore. Something is blocking my magic flow. I'll probably have to pry it open or make the magic particles even smaller to permeate the barrier.

As these thoughts run through my mind, I feel something rush toward the classroom.

"It's here...," I say ominously, just because.

At that moment, I hear an explosion. The door flies off its hinges, and my classmates fall into a frenzy. Just then, men in black burst into the room with drawn swords.

"All of you, don't move! We are the Shadow Garden, and we're taking over this school!" they scream, blocking the entrance.

"Are you serious...?" My groan is muted by the clamor around me.

The students can't move.

Maybe this is some kind of special training or a prank...or it was real. Most of the students can't grasp that the Academy for Dark Knights is under attack.

I'm the only one who completely understands what's happening. I'm the only one who knows they're serious, that they're blocking our magic, and that the same thing is happening in all the other classrooms.

"Incredible...," I involuntarily utter in awe.

These guys did it. I mean, they're *really* going for it. They're doing what all the boys in the world dream about, what fills a page in the fantasies of boyhood adolescence.

* * *

They're reenacting the scenario where terrorists take over the school!

I'm so moved, I'm shaking.

I can't tell you how many times I've imagined this scene. Hundreds, thousands…millions of times. I've thought out countless iterations, and right before me, my dream is coming to life.

"Stay in your seats! Put your hands up!" The men in jet-black swing their swords to threaten the students, who are slowly piecing together the situation.

They must be high-spec professionals with a cult following. I mean, they chose to side with terrorists.

But the focus is, of course, on the student protagonists.

What will they do?

How will they act?

The possibilities are endless.

"You seem to have no idea where you are," echoes a gallant voice across the room. A girl with a sword on her waist has confronted them.

"Take over the Academy for Dark Knights? You must be out of your mind."

Rose Oriana is standing up to them, completely alone.

"I think we asked you to put down the weapon, missy."

"No." She wields her rapier.

"Hmph. You'll be a good lesson for the others." He readies his katana.

This is bad.

She hasn't realized she can't use magic.

"…What in the—?" With her sword at the ready, her face turns a perplexed shade of red.

"Seems you've finally caught on." He sneers behind his mask.

At this rate, this is going to be really, really bad.

"But you're too late."

The all-black blade plummets toward Rose. She can't possibly defend herself with her magic restrained.

I kick a chair over and run.

"—…nr!"

Stop. Don't do that. I process the situation at a breakneck speed, and the world around me slows down. I'm both exhausted and furious in this moment.

"…Aaaah!"

If this continues, she'll be the first person killed by the terrorists.

And that can't happen. I won't let it.

"Aaaaaaaah, AAAAAAH!!"

To be the first victim of these terrorists…is my duty…as an extra!

"Stooooooooopppppppppppppppp!!" I let out a soul-wrenching howl as I leap between them.

As she watches the bare blade draw closer to her, Rose knows this is the end.

Her fragile body can't tame the magic. Neither can she block nor evade the attack. She tries to twist her torso to lighten the blow, but even that movement is frustratingly sluggish.

She won't make it in time.

Her death has come. That's reality.

At that moment, a shout rings out that she can feel in her eardrums.

"Stooooooooopppppppppppppppp!!"

Something shoves her out of the way.

"Aaah…!" She instantly switches to a defensive posture as she crashes to the floor. When she gets up, her eyes fill with a shocking view.

"What the hell…?"

In front of her…a stricken boy is lying helplessly on the floor. She can clearly see the pool of blood beneath him growing larger and larger.

He's sustained a fatal wound.

"Nooooooooooooo!!" A scream reverberates through the classroom.

Indifferent to the blood staining her clothes, Rose cradles the boy in her arms—the one who's recently left a deep impression on her.

"Cid Kagenou…," Rose murmurs. The boy slightly opens his eyes. "You idiot. Why did you protect me?"

They only met the other day. They've never even spoken properly to each other. She can't imagine why he risked his life to save her.

The boy opens his mouth. "Gack, kaff!"

He vomits a stream of blood.

"Cid!"

His hacked-up blood splatters across her porcelain cheeks, and he smiles at her…before drawing his last breath. He wears the dying expression of a man who completed his mission.

"Why…?"

A tear cascades down her face. She stops herself from weeping as she holds him in her arms. When she looks at the dead boy's face, she feels as if she's figured everything out.

She knows why he was so strangely persistent during the preliminaries.

She knows why his eyes burned when he gazed at her.

And she knows why he laid down his life to protect her.

They are all connected.

Rose isn't dumb. Ever since she was young, she's had suitors chasing after her for being a beautiful princess. But she's never been pursued with this much fervor before. No suitor ever loved her enough to sacrifice his life.

"Thank you…"

She can never tell him how she felt, but she vows to avenge him.

"Let this be a valuable lesson for you." The man in jet-black stands before Rose.

"—…h!" Rose bites down on her lower lip and glares up at him.

"Still thinking of defying us, huh."

"Tch… I'll obey your orders." Rose hangs her head, knowing it isn't yet the time to get her revenge.

"Hmm. Head to the auditorium!" the men in black order, making their move.

They get the students to stand, shackle their hands one behind the other, and lead them out of the room. No one dares to resist.

Two male students at the end of the line turn back toward the classroom.

"Cid…"

"Poor Cid…"

The boys stare at his stiff face, looking as if they have more to say.

"Keep it moving."

The terrorists force the duo out of the classroom. The sound of footsteps in the hallway grows distant. It's silent again.

And then, the arm of the alleged corpse begins twitching.

When I confirm the classroom is clear, I pound on my chest.

Beat! Beat, dammit!

I hit myself over and over, forcing myself to suck in air.

Up and at 'em!!

Until…

"Koff, hack, gak!"

It stirs, and my once-stopped heart starts pumping again.

This is another esoteric technique, Ten-Minute Death: Heartbreak Mob.

With this technique, I let tiny magic particles trickle into my brain from my stopped heart, preserving blood flow and allowing me to stay in cardiac arrest for a long time without any consequences. It's a risky technique: One slipup, and I go to the other side. But sometimes, I have to endanger my life for the art of performance. And that's what happened today. Nothing more, nothing less.

"Oww…"

I check the gash on my back. I let him cut me because I knew I might be examined up close. I avoided getting fatally injured, of course, but it was deep enough to be convincing.

I try using my magic to heal myself. It looks like my magic can get around the barrier if I process it in teeny-tiny amounts. Alternatively, if I apply pressure and release magic, I think I'll be able to remove the membrane by force.

"Good enough for now."

It'll take too long for them to completely heal, and I'll be in a tough spot if someone catches me in the act. I heal to the point where I have no trouble moving, and with my trusty "I-somehow-miraculously survived" routine, I should be good to go.

"All right," I grunt, rising to my feet.

I make sure I can control my body and magic, wiping the blood off my face and straightening the wrinkles out of my school uniform.

The white curtains ripple in the midday breeze that flows through the window. As they billow and fall, the patches of bright sunlight and black shadows change form.

The fallen chairs and scattered desks. The broken door and bloody ground. The sight announces the end of a normal life.

I close my eyes and take a deep breath.

"All right. Let's go."

I leave the classroom and start down the empty, silent hallway.

Sherry Barnett is too focused on deciphering the pendant-shaped artifact to notice the commotion right away.

"This is…"

She picks it up and studies it up close, noticing something and narrowing her light-pink eyes.

"This…can't be."

Her gaze remains focused on the artifact as her pen begins twirling across the paper.

She doesn't seem cognizant of the chaos around her. The explosive sounds, the footsteps in the hallway—all of this is beyond her scope of awareness.

"What's going on?"

"Someone is attacking the school."

"You can't use magic, so don't be careless."

Even the conversation between the two knights doesn't reach her ears.

"But how…? There's no way…"

She's completely fixated on the artifact. She tends to forget her surroundings during her research, but it's never been this extreme. There's something important about that relic that's captured her attention.

Her quill makes crisp movements across the paper.

Those light-pink eyes come one step closer to uncovering the truth.

At that moment, a man in jet-black comes crashing through the window of the lab. Flying shards of glass leave small cuts on Sherry's face.

"What the…?!"

"Who goes there?!"

The two knights ready their swords. The stinging sensation in her cheeks finally makes Sherry aware of the situation.

"Huh? What?"

She grabs the artifact and crawls under her desk to hide. After touching her cheek, she finds a little blood on her hand.

"We are the Shadow Garden. Or was it the Shadow Guardian? Oh, who gives a crap. I'm Rex. Rex, the Game of Betrayal." He scoffs behind his mask. "This thing is such a nuisance."

He flings his mask aside, revealing a flippant man with dull red hair, laughing with the eyes of a starving, feral dog.

"Eek." The mask lands near Sherry's feet, causing her to back away, still concealed.

"You're the Shadow Garden I've heard so damn much about…"

"I don't know your motives, but did you really think you could get away with attacking the school?"

Rex chuckles. "I guess that'd be too easy. Oh, the Shadow Garden has it tough. By the way..." He stops midsentence. "I forgot why we're attacking."

He cackles evilly.

"Stop messing around."

"Oh, but I'm serious. Though that doesn't matter. My job is to acquire the artifact. Once I have it, you can struggle and squirm to your heart's content..."

Rex narrows his eyes sharply.

"Do you know where it is?" He glares at the knights.

"...I have no idea what you're talking about."

"We know nothing."

Rex smiles from ear to ear. "Your faces tell me otherwise...!"

The air quivers, and his magic overpowers the room.

"A—...!" Sherry clasps her hands over her mouth to prevent herself from screaming as she crawls. It's just a bit farther to the door.

"So who wants to go first?" Rex's ravenous, feral gaze scours the room. "Let's start with the girl."

He disappears into thin air.

That's when Sherry realizes he's standing before her.

"Aaaaaaahhhh!"

"Farewell."

"No!" Sherry closes her eyes as she covers her head, huddling.

"I won't let you!"

The sword hurls toward her and strikes the floor.

Sherry fearfully peeks through her clenched eyes to find a stocky knight—with a beard as bushy as a lion's mane—standing in front of her with his sword at the ready.

"Ooh, impressive. Considering you're working without magic."

"Magic isn't everything. If I'm fighting a weakling, I can easily dodge any attack."

"Weakling...? Damn buffoon. Do you really think you're stronger than me?" Rex ferociously scowls at the large man.

"I do."

"Why don't you tell me your name?"

"I am Glen, the Lion's Mane, vice commander of the Crimson Order."

Another knight lines up next to him.

"I'm Marco of the Crimson Order."

"I didn't ask you."

In that last moment, Marco looks down at Sherry.

"Run."

With that, the battle begins.

Sherry crawls into the hallway and proceeds to sprint at full speed. She covers her ears to muffle the bloodcurdling screams behind her.

I walk onto the rooftop and peer down at the campus.

I can see all the faculty bound up by the auditorium, which is a massive hall that can easily fit all the students. It's where the school hosts its entrance ceremonies and the occasional lecture by a public figure or a theatrical performance.

The Knight Order has gathered outside the campus in response to the commotion, but there's a clear threshold beyond which they aren't advancing. That could be the boundary of whatever's blocking everyone's magic. There didn't seem to be any students left in the school buildings, just men in black scrounging for anyone still hiding.

I scoff as I look down at the school.

I've always wanted to do this.

I peer at the ravaged school, the shackled students, and the mysterious terrorist organization. I can cross this off my bucket list.

Gaze down at the campus from the rooftop. Check.

Well, I guess I'll have some fun before it gets dark. The truth is, I realized something when the men in jet-black barged into class.

They have no sense of style.

Imagine a light breeze, a clear blue sky, a sunny afternoon—and someone coming out onstage in a long black cloak. Who does that?

Unheard of.

They made one dire mistake. Right… They've underestimated the importance of TPO: There's a Time, Place, and Occasion for everything. If you don't adhere to it, fashion sense will be totally out of whack. Their disregard for TPO is tacky. I mean, black cloaks should *only* be worn at night.

I'm planning on taking them out nice and slow; time isn't an issue. I would rather hold out and savor the fun.

Which is why I'm going with the strategy Operation: Slow 'n' Steady Till Nightfall.

I'm thinking all this as I observe the campus when I spot two men in black walking down the corridors. Yuck, wearing jet-black on a sunny day? Talk about uncool.

Yeah…they make me want to play sniper.

I slice off a thumb-size piece of slime from my suit. I roll it into a ball, infuse it with magic, lay it on the rooftop, and prepare to give it a good flick.

"You're in my line of fire, you dummies," I mutter to myself, then send it flying.

Whiz. Zooming through the air, my slime ball zips through one of their skulls.

"Augh…"

In the same way, I pierce the second man's heart. I've already defeated them in two hits. Unbelievable. I'm bummed. I was in the mood to launch one more.

"Oh well. My next target is…"

With my slime bomb at the ready, I close one eye to scope out my next victim.

In the school building across from me, I spot a defenseless blockhead.

"Target acquired. It's a girl with light-pink hair… Wait, what?"

That's Sherry.

What's she doing over there? She's giving herself away by blatantly looking back after each step.

"Sherry, you're blowing your cover."

I confirm that a man in black is lunging at Sherry from behind. I lock onto my slime bomb target…and shoot.

Whir.

The man's head flies off.

"Mission complete."

Completely oblivious, Sherry keeps moving until she disappears from view.

Hmm. I wonder what's up.

My normie senses are tingling, telling me there's a major cutscene about to happen. And then, right around the climax, I shall grace the stage as the mastermind behind it all…

Ooh, I can't wait.

Okay, here I go. I infuse my legs with magic and bound into the air when no one's looking.

"Yahoo!"

I safely land on the school building across the way. After that, I jump down, grab hold of a window ledge, and swing into the building. I glance around the hallway…and there she is.

The girl with light-pink hair looks around like a gopher.

"Like I said, you're blowing your cover."

There's a man in jet-black behind Sherry. Right before he grabs her, I rush at him at full speed.

"Huh?" Sherry senses something moving and looks behind her.

She hears a *whoosh*…but no one is there. A silent hallway extends into the distance.

"Maybe I'm just paranoid…?"

Sherry cautiously peers around her, her shoes lightly tapping against the floor. She presses the artifact against her chest.

Just a moment ago, the knights said they couldn't use magic. If that's true, it would mean it has something to do with her, and she might know what caused it. And in terms of the artifact…

Sherry hugs it tightly one more time.

"I've got to do something about this…!"

The image of the two knights bravely fighting to help her escape floats into her mind. She knows she can't let them die in vain.

Wrestling with these thoughts, she turns the corner.

"Ack!"

There's a man in black. Sherry panics and attempts to conceal herself.

She thinks she's done for. She swears they lock eyes.

There's another *whish*.

"It's fine. I'm still good… I haven't been caught…" Sherry prays as she looks ahead once more… "Phew, I'm still safe…"

Her ebony assailant has vanished.

She bravely yet cautiously surveys the area while her shoes tap rhythmically on the floor.

"Oh!"

Another of the enemies gazes down the hall from the classroom window.

Sherry tries to hide in a frenzy, but it's too late. The door swings open to reveal the man in jet-black.

"Eep!" Sherry covers her head and closes her eyes.

…

……

Another *whiz*.

"What?" Upon nervously opening her eyes, she finds he's gone.

"Phew. They haven't found me…"

Sherry braces herself even more as her feet softly patter against the floor. She checks every inch of the hallway, the classrooms, and, most obviously, behind her. Her eyes flicker left and right. She's surveying the area when she trips over herself.

"Oof!" She crashes on the ground, looking up in time to see the artifact whirling into the air.

"Ahhh!"

It's about to crash onto the floor…when someone catches it. Sherry glances up to find her newest friend.

"Cid!"

But he's covered in blood.

"Are you okay?! You're hurt…"

"Don't worry about it. I miraculously escaped death. No biggie."

He seems exhausted for some reason and stares at Sherry through half-closed eyes.

"I've got to tell you a few things. Like, you've gotta stop talking to yourself. And thinking while you're walking. And you should watch your step."

He lets out a deep sigh.

"And your tap-tap-tapping down the hall is super-loud. Let's start with taking off your loafers."

Sherry nods in response.

I guard Sherry as we head to the back end of the first floor into the assistant principal's office. Oh, and I secretly kill five more of them along the way.

We open a thick door and walk in.

There's a tasteful lounge in the center of the room and an entire wall stacked with oversized books. Files are piled high on a desk in the back. Sunlight gently pours in from the northern window. It's obviously a space for proper adults.

Sherry sits at a desk she seems to know well and rummages through the drawers.

"Try not to make so much noise."

Her light-pink hair sways as she obediently nods.

"Whew." I lie across the love seat and take a deep breath.

I'm beat.

I know Sherry is the main character, but there's no way this is going to work out. She won't be able to beat the Final Boss. Under these circumstances, it's normal for the character to have a sidekick, but I don't sense any allies around here. It's a flawed scenario.

But after significant consideration, I've decided to intervene as the savior type of background character. I'm an extra who will never act where others can see—never ever.

"Found it." Sherry comes back from the desk with a pile of documents, spreading them across the coffee table.

"What's this?" I don't know anything about these strange alphabets, landforms, or formulas.

"This artifact is called the Eye of Avarice. I believe this is what's currently blocking our magic."

She shows me a sketch of an ominous-looking sphere that's the size of a Ping-Pong ball.

"The Eye absorbs and collects the magic around it. When it's activated, it's harder to hone magic in the area."

"But the men in black had no problems using magic."

"They must have programmed the Eye to recognize their magical wavelength. I've already confirmed it doesn't consume preregistered magic. It also has difficulties absorbing microscopic particles with powerful energy, but neither of us would recognize those in the first place."

Hey.

"And as if that's not troubling enough, it can also use the magic stored inside it. I'm guessing they were originally planning to use this artifact as a weapon, but it can't store magic for long periods. I believe it's defective."

"But it's effective in the short-term, even if it can't store the power very long."

"Correct. Right now, there are hundreds of dark knights held hostage in the auditorium. In theory, if they released the magic in the artifact... they might just be able to obliterate the school."

"Whoa..."

"I was the first one to decode the Eye with my research. When I realized its potential dangers, I kept it away from the world of academia and asked the kingdom to store it for safekeeping... Oh, why did this happen?" Sherry looks at me with gentle eyes.

"It's either a replica or it was stolen. Is there a way to operate it?"

"Yes." Sherry nods and produces a large pendant.

"That's a real dirty pendant you got there."

"This seems to control it. The Eye cannot move on its own; I believe it can only be used when attached to this device. When they act together, the artifact is no longer defective and is limited to storing magic short-term."

"It'll be able to hold magic for longer?"

"I would have to put them together and experiment to know for sure. But yes, I believe it's possible."

"Huh."

"This device has the power to temporarily disable the Eye. We should be able to free the people in the auditorium in that time."

"Sounds good. And then?"

"Well, I haven't finished examining the artifact, so I'd like to prioritize that."

"I see."

"After I interpret it, we can bring the activated artifact closer to the Eye."

"How?"

"Um...they're vigilantly patrolling the ground level, so I think we might have to get closer underground." Sherry smiles somewhat nervously.

"Underground?"

"Yes." Sherry takes a few books off the bookshelf, and it swings back to reveal a staircase leading to a lower level.

"Neat."

I love these kinds of gimmicks.

"There are still a few hidden escape tunnels left in some of the on-campus facilities, but no one's used this passage in a while."

There's a hint of sadness in her eyes.

"The stairs are dusty…and there aren't any footprints. I wish my foster father had escaped though here…"

"Ah, Assistant Principal Lutheran. He adopted you, right?"

"He used to help my mother with her research, and he's taken care of me for as long as I can remember. Even after Mother died and I had nowhere to go, he took me under his wing and raised me as his own."

"Sounds like a great guy."

"Yes, he really is. He's always the one saving me…and this time, I want to be the one to save him." Sherry beams.

"I hope he's all right. After we get closer underground, what should we do?"

"Oh, um…we go through the tunnels and throw the active artifact into the auditorium."

"Won't it break?"

"Even if it does, it'll still disable the Eye temporarily. All we'll need is the dark knights to give us a hand…"

The climax sounds a bit weak, but I could spice it right up if I turn into Shadow and go on a rampage. To tell you the truth, I'm thankful she prepared a great scene for me to show off what I can do.

"Fantastic. Let's do it."

"Great! I'll just hurry up and finish deciphering this."

"My back hurts, so I can't help too much. But good luck."

I'm glad she has a decent tactic. I guess I won't have to be the supporting side character after all.

"Cid, don't overdo it. I'll do the best I can. I've never been able to help anyone, but now it's my turn to save my foster father and everyone else."

"Yeah, you got this. Oh, I'll be right back—gotta go to the bathroom."

I leave Sherry to her research so I can go out and play.

With the wild eyes of a starving dog, Rex opens the auditorium doors and boldly saunters through the room. A group of men follow.

The students are forced to stay in their chairs, lowering their heads when the group approaches them. There are three floors in the enormous, drafty auditorium, and all of the exits are guarded by men enshrouded in jet-black. The students are being monitored and not allowed to make a single peep. An insincere smile plays on Rex's face as he slips out of the auditorium and heads toward a waiting room.

"How was it?" asks a man in black as soon as Rex shuts the door.

His voice is deep and dignified. Even though he hides his face with a mask and is dressed like the others, his superiority is instantly recognizable.

"You don't waste time, do you, Sir Gaunt? We've almost completely taken over the school. The Knight Order is making a ruckus outside, but they're not even worth our breath."

"Irrelevant. I'm asking whether you've obtained the artifact."

"Oh, the artifact. About that..." Rex shrugs as he looks at Sir Gaunt. "I'm pretty sure it's in that young girl's possession. You know, the one with peach hair."

"Are you saying you couldn't retrieve it?"

Rex scratches his head and averts his gaze. "Well, I guess."

"Quit screwing around." Sir Gaunt's magic heightens, and the surrounding air undulates under its pressure.

Rex's cheeks go stiff as he feels the knight's bloodlust. "Take it easy. I've secured its general location and shall be retrieving it soon."

"Your antics are interfering with my plans. The next time you screw up, I'm taking your head. How's that?"

"All right, I get it."

Sir Gaunt's piercing eyes follow Rex, who's heading toward the door with his hands lifted above his head.

"Oh, almost forgot." Rex stops before making his exit. "We may have trouble."

He looks back to see Sir Gaunt's reaction and receives the cue to continue.

"A bunch of Thirds have been slain. Two of the Seconds are dead. One man's heart has been crushed, and the other had a small incision in his pressure points. My best guess is the latter was stabbed by a rapier. All of them were only struck once. The enemy seems dexterous," comments Rex, sniggering like a ravenous wolf.

"Well, well...perhaps it's the Shadow Garden. The bait has finally worked."

"Seems that way. You might want to watch your back."

"Keh-heh... You think a man like me needs to be cautious?"

"Oh, I think you'll be just fine, Mr. Ex-Rounds."

"Hmph. Make sure to bring the Shadow Garden's heads along with the artifact."

"That goes without saying." Rex leaves the room with the corner of his lips curled into a grin.

Sir Gaunt sneers to himself. "Finally, everything will fall into place..." He takes the ominous artifact out of his breast pocket and stares at it suspiciously.

"This will mark my return to the Rounds."

The man continues snickering to himself creepily.

When Rex and his subordinates are walking through the corridor, something strange suddenly attacks them while they're searching for the artifact. Rex's subordinate vanishes before his eyes.

"What the—?"

Rex scans the area to determine what it was, but there aren't any suspicious shadows around him. The only hint he has is a *whoosh* in the air.

Buzz, zip. A sound slices through space.

"Nng...!"

And the lackey next to Rex is gone.

But this time, he manages to catch a glimpse of it. There was a boy in a school uniform—drenched in blood. Using the heel of his palm, the boy knocked the man out and stole him away.

Rex powers up, intensifying his vision to its limit and focusing his gaze. Only then can he detect these rapid movements.

"Stay alert! Enemy!" Rex shouts, vigilantly scoping the area. "...Oh?"

He stands in place, bewildered.

The subordinates who were at his back are gone. Before he's realized it, he's standing alone in the corridor.

Then there's a *whiz.*

Hearing it, Rex immediately channels all his strength into protecting his heart.

"Guh...!"

The heel of someone's palm hits his arm.

Crack. The force of it snaps Rex's bones and sends him flying backward.

"That...little shit!!" Rex promptly resets his stance and brandishes his sword.

But no one's there. He clucks his tongue in frustration.

A single palm strike has broken the bones in his left arm, which he'd been protecting with magic. His heart might have shattered if he hadn't shielded himself when he did.

Whish. Rex moves with the noise, tuning in to the presence behind him and swinging. His timing is perfect.

The runt...is getting faster! How dare he! Rex takes stabs at the air behind the boy, quickly resuming his posture with the sole aim of protecting his heart.

"Agh...!"

He suffers a blow to the ribs.

Rex jumps back to reduce the impact as he tracks the boy with his eyes. He can barely make out his afterimage.

"Ts..." Rex hacks out a mix of saliva and blood and stands on the defensive.

It's nearly impossible to detect the enemy, and countering is out of the question. Only he's taking damage. From an objective standpoint, there's no graver situation. But...Rex has a wealth of experience worming himself out from between a rock and a hard place.

For he is Rex, a Named Child.

"That's a handy artifact you're using," Rex comments so his enemy can hear.

He's figured out the enemy's shtick.

It doesn't take him long to piece it together. His opponent moves faster than humanly possible, which means he requires extraordinary power to keep it up.

"At first glance, I have the disadvantage. But you can't fool me. You're pushing yourself, right?"

With inhuman speed comes sacrifice. He sees the traces of it already.

"Don't you know your uniform is covered in blood?"

Yes...Rex solved the riddle when he saw the red uniform: His opponent used the power of the artifact to achieve logic-defying speeds. And in exchange, it's wearing him down. It's clear from the rivers of blood pouring out of his enemy. The boy will reach his limit. If Rex can hold out until then...victory is his.

That's Rex, the Game of Betrayal, the Named Child, who can completely expose his victims with minimal information.

"I'd guess that you have a few hits left. That's when you'll have reached your limit!" Rex declares in a powerful voice.

But his enemy doesn't reply. He's been silent and still ever since Rex started his little speech.

"Guess I've hit the nail on the head." The corners of Rex's lips form a sinister smile.

He can see his victory. But...it's not as easy as Rex makes it out to be. In fact, he still has to evade the undetectable palm strike a few more times.

"Hey, why so silent?" Rex starts feeling confident, refusing to show any sign of weakness.

This battle is one of…intense psychological warfare.

"Come out, you chicken!"

Whoosh.

Just as the sound rushes through the air, Rex evades the attack using only his instincts, twisting his upper body to avoid the trajectory of his hand.

That fast?! He uses his right arm as a shield at the very last second.

"Gaaaah!!"

It snaps in every possible place. He backs away, retaining his grip on his sword through sheer determination.

And yet, his opponent persists. Rex has only seen the enemy's most basic moves, and he's drawing near.

In other words…this is the turning point in their battle.

"Come at meeeeeeeeee!!" Rex shrieks as he protects his weak points.

His enemy has reached his limit. If Rex can endure this final strike, victory is his.

Seconds later, a palm slams into his stomach.

"Gah!! Aaaaaghhhh!!"

Rex vomits a stream of blood as he's thrown backward. He blasts through the wall into a classroom, tumbling into desks and chairs before crashing onto the ground.

"Kah-kah…!" Clutching his stomach, he coughs up blood. His ribs tear his internal organs.

But…he's alive. Guarding with all his might pays off.

"Heh-heh…" Rex's bloody lips curl into a sneer as he lifts his head.

That's when he sees them.

"The hell is this…?"

Corpses lie in a heap in the classroom.

All of them are men in black. It's clear they hardly bear any wounds; each was slain with a single attack.

Did that one child kill all these Named Children by himself…?

Tap, tap, tap.

He hears someone walking toward him in the hallway.

Tap, tap.

The sound of footsteps ceases at the doorway.

Silence.

Rex notices the palm gripping his sword is abnormally sweaty.

Click. The doorknob turns and breaks the silence.

Then...the entrance opens.

There's no one there.

With a *whir*, Rex's right arm is ripped to pieces.

Another hum, and his left arm is torn off.

Whoosh.

Whish.

Whiz.

And so it goes.

Every time there's a sound, Rex loses more flesh.

"AAAAAAGH... Aaaaaaaghhhh...aghh..."

Right before his head whirls into the air, Rex realizes the boy possesses an infinite amount of power.

"You're doing great."

That's the voice Rex hears when he dies.

In the ransacked lab, Nu looks down at a corpse. With dark-brown eyes and matching hair, Nu wears a pair of frumpy glasses and the uniform for the Academy of Science as a disguise to blend in, but she can't hide her sensuality.

"You're Glen, the Lion's Mane, from the Crimson Order."

The corpse glares into space, wearing an anguished expression. He seems to have suffered profoundly. Without magic, he whose name is known throughout the Knight Order is feeble.

Nu's attention is directed elsewhere. There's one more knight in the room, and he's still breathing.

"Marco Granger. You joined the Crimson Order."

Nu recognizes his face, which is handsome with luscious blue hair.

Not only is he one of the strongest dark knights, but he is also rumored to be the future commander of the Order. She remembers him having a strong sense of justice.

Marco was supposed to be Nu's husband in their arranged marriage.

They sent many letters to each other and shared dances at the ball. But in the end, he was nothing but the man her parents chose for her. She never knew how he felt about the situation, but she could never bring herself to love him.

But she doesn't necessarily hate him. She may not have loved him, but she thought he was kind. She wouldn't have minded marrying him one day. She imagines that tying the knot with a respectable man would have led to a bright future.

An arranged path, an arranged partner, an arranged future.

Nu never used to have much of an opinion. In the past, she conformed to the values of those around her and lived as per their dictates. She didn't mind at the time. But looking back on it now, she finds that lifestyle terribly confining.

As she gazes at his face, she suddenly remembers the ball. Nu wryly smiles as she recalls showing off Marco's attractive face around it like some kind of accessory.

Somehow, memories always stick with us the more we try to forget about them.

"What's up, Nu?"

She hears a voice behind her and turns. That she hasn't sensed him doesn't surprise her. She knows him by his voice.

"Master Shadow…"

She didn't notice that an average-looking black-haired boy had entered the lab. He walks past Nu and flings open one cabinet after another.

"This used to be my arranged fiancé."

"Oh. What will you do?"

"I personally have no reason to kill him or keep him alive."

"And that's fine," he replies, rummaging through the cabinets and continuing his search.

Nu leaves Marco's side and stands next to the boy. "Master Shadow, I know it's a bit late, but I have something to report."

"Go ahead."

"The Shadow Garden has infiltrated the campus. We're waiting on standby and will move at your command."

"Got it."

"But fighting when our magic is blocked comes with a risk. Only the Seven Shadows can operate at their usual speed, but the only one of them in the capital is Lady Gamma. And…well, this kind of thing isn't her strong suit…"

"She's got no game."

"Um…correct. As for me, I-I'm only at about half my normal strength…"

"I see."

"Lady Gamma is currently leading the entire organization. She's suggested they won't be in control of our magic for much longer and that we should wait it out until then."

"All right."

"The men in jet-black are holed up in the auditorium and haven't moved. At the moment, they don't seem to have any demands. The Knight Order has the campus surrounded, but Iris Midgar and the other commanders are the only ones strong enough to take them on. Given that they weren't fond of us in peaceful times, I don't think they'll lend us a hand."

"Okay."

"Master Shadow. We'll stay on standby until further orders."

"Okay."

"Is that all right?"

"Okay… Oh, wait a sec."

"Sure."

"I'm looking for a few things. I need mithril tweezers, the bone powder of earth dragons, and the enchanted stone of ash…"

Nu retrieves each item from the cabinet.

"Thanks. Whew, you saved my butt."

"My pleasure. May I ask what they're for?"

He holds the various items in both arms. "Oh, this stuff? I'm going to use this to alter the artifact."

"Alter the artifact, huh?" Nu parrots.

She couldn't have guessed in a million years that he was so well versed in artifacts, but it wouldn't be odd for him to know such things. Why would he want to alter it in this dire situation?

"Something called the Eye of Avarice is impeding our magic. I'm currently making the final adjustments to a different artifact to temporarily disable it."

"Incredible… You never let us down."

She's stunned. Not only has he identified the source blocking their magic, he's even preparing to nullify it. Plus, disabling a powerful artifact requires extraordinary knowledge. Without the wisdom of one of the greatest minds in the nation, this is an impossible feat. She shudders in the presence of his limitless mind.

"I should be done around sunset."

"Understood. We'll be ready to mobilize when it's complete."

"I can't wait."

"Yes."

Nu watches him leave the room with his items before checking to see if her ex-fiancé is still conscious.

She runs her ebony blade down the nape of his neck.

His breathing and pulse are normal—stable. He's alive but clearly unconscious.

"I'll spare you your life."

Nu leaves a shallow cut in his neck and disappears.

"I'm back."

Upon seeing Cid return with the ingredients, Sherry smiles, retrieving them from him and lining them up on her desk.

"Thank you so much. I should be able to finish it now."

"Good luck."

Sherry quickly sets to work on the artifact. Cid is lying on the sofa, reading a book.

It's silent for a while.

The light that flows in through the window slowly turns vermilion.

Cid occasionally gets up to go to the bathroom. When Sherry offers him medicine to relieve his upset stomach given his frequent visits, he accepts it with a complicated expression.

Time passes, and the sun begins to set. The red hue intensifies, and the shadows grow darker. When Sherry turns on the lantern, everything becomes a shade darker outside the room. She finally approaches the end of her task around sunset.

"I'm done." Sherry holds up the pendant and shows it to Cid.

"It's amazing."

"Thank you. It's the best I could do."

"Yeah, and it's nice that it's just after sunset. The future of the school depends on you." Cid stands up and pats Sherry on the back. "I can't help you anymore. You must save the world with your own hands."

"I-I'll do my best," she says nervously, picking up the lantern and facing the stairs. "My sincerest gratitude. Thanks to you, I'll be able to rescue my foster father." Sherry glances back at him once more, then lowers her head.

"It was nothing. I hope he's okay."

"Thanks." Sherry grins and descends.

After a long trip down the damp staircase, she arrives at the bottom. The air is completely different down here. The dark tunnels are illuminated by the light from her lantern, and the paths start forking off: One wrong move, and she'll never reach her destination.

"Erm..." Sherry takes out her map to confirm the path to the auditorium.

"Go straight and then take a left at the third turn..."

At first, she timidly scampers down the path.

But then she remembers having walked these tunnels with her foster father. Even though she pestered him while he was working, he came down to play with her anyway. This is an incredibly precious memory to Sherry.

The young woman doesn't remember her biological father. He died soon after she was born. And the memory of her mother has almost entirely faded from her mind. Her mother was murdered during a robbery one night when Sherry was only nine years old.

Sherry remembers the black shadow she saw through the crack between the closet door. Her dreams were occasionally plagued by her mother's screams and the sound of ghastly laughter.

For many years after the incident, Sherry couldn't speak. She rejected those around her, instead choosing to work on the artifact her mother left behind. As if following in her footsteps, Sherry devoted herself to research.

Her foster father was her savior. He took her in, supported her research, and gave her a loving family. Through that, Sherry finally regained her voice. Almost all her memories of family are of him.

Her entire life, she's been supported by her foster father. And now it's time to repay him.

"I've got to keep going."

Sherry walks the dark path alone. Her steps are no longer frightened or timid.

It isn't long before she arrives.

"I think I'm under the auditorium…"

The single path split into many: the path to the first floor, then the middle, then up to the second floor…

She follows her map.

"Oh…!"

She's found it.

It's a small air vent running between the second and third floors. While it can't fit a person, there's plenty of room for her to toss the pendant inside.

Sherry furtively peers through the vent to see what's happening.

She remembers Cid's words: When in hiding, it's important to release the tension in the body—to breathe slowly and relax.

There are hundreds of students sitting in the auditorium and a few instructors, who were present nonetheless. Then there are a handful of men in black. Sherry believes all the hostages can escape once their magic is free.

She's ready.

First, she steps away from the vent and takes out the pendant. When she connects it to the enchanted stone, a white light and shining letters float in the air.

Sherry tosses the glowing pendant into the air vent without hesitation.

All I know is I've admired shadowbrokers for as long as I can remember.

Was it a certain anime? Or was it a manga—or a movie?

Eh, I guess it doesn't matter. I was all in for anything that featured a mastermind, or an eminence in shadow, as I like to call them. These characters were never the protagonists or final bosses but were relegated to a role behind the scenes where they flaunted their powers and meddled in the affairs of others. I've always looked up to the men in the shadows.

I wanted to be one of them.

Think of children who worship their favorite superheroes.

That was me but with master puppeteers.

The Eminence in Shadow

nestly can't remember what catalyzed this desire.

know is I've admired shadowbrokers for as long as
remember.

it a certain anime? Or was it a manga—or a movie?

guess it doesn't matter. I was all in for anything that featured a
ermind, or an eminence in shadow, as I like to call them. These
acters were never the protagonists or final bosses but were relegated to a role
nd the scenes where they flaunted their powers and meddled in the
rs of others. I've always looked up to the men in the shadows.
nted to be one of them.

My Idea of the Ultimate Shadow Commander!

Final Chapter

The Eminence in Shadow

Final Chapter

Rose observes the men in black with her honey-colored eyes.

It's been several hours since she's been brought to the auditorium. The sun has already set, and the warm light from the ceiling illuminates the auditorium.

She's cut the restraints off her arms with a small concealed knife. Keeping up the pretense of being bound to her chair, she passes the knife to a girl in the Student Council, who then hands it off to the next student in line.

Rose can move at any time, but she's fully aware that acting now would be a waste.

Her enemies may be few, but they're all too powerful to neglect. Plus, they're terribly efficient. Of the group, a man known as Rex and his superior officer, Sir Gaunt, are immensely stronger than the rest. The professors who underestimated and opposed them have been helplessly slain. Even if the hostages could use magic, their chances of winning would be questionable.

Luckily, Rex hasn't been back in a while. She hopes the Knight Order has slaughtered him outside...but she knows a fierce warrior can't be taken down so easily. Rose's honest thought is that she needs to improve the situation somehow before he returns.

While Sir Gaunt spends most of his time in the waiting room, he occasionally shows up in the auditorium to search for Rex, at whom he curses under his breath for his prolonged absence. Judging by his appearance and dense magic, Rose believes he can surpass an expert fighter. He might even be able to topple Iris Midgar...not that she wants to believe it. If that's true, Rose's chances of defeating him—even if she regains her magic—are remarkably low to none.

In any case, Rose knows it isn't the right moment to move yet. But the truth of the situation is she has no time.

As the minutes elapse, Rose can feel magic slipping out of her body. She doesn't know the reason, but her best guess is that it's related to the phenomenon that blocks it. Even though Rose is far from feeling weak, the students with less magic are starting to feel sick. In a few more hours, some of them may even suffer from magic deficiency, which means they'll lose the chance to fight back forever.

There's a figure who always suppressed panic and unease as it rose in his chest.

Every time Rose remembers the heroic stance of the boy who sacrificed himself to save her, a burning sensation rises up in her body. She isn't going to let his wishes be forgotten. As she repeats this promise to herself, she waits for her time to come.

And just then, the moment arrives, unexpectedly.

The auditorium is suddenly lit up by a radiant white light.

Rose doesn't know what it is, but she reacts before she can think.

She couldn't care less where it came from. Her instincts are telling her this is her final chance.

While everyone is captivated by the blinding light, Rose squints as she rushes toward one of her captors. The moment she wraps her hands around his unguarded neck, Rose has a realization.

I can use magic! She chops his head off with her hand.

Rose doesn't know why she can use magic again, but it doesn't matter. She snatches the sword from the waist of the headless man.

Raising it, she howls. "We've got our magic back! Everyone, rise! This is our time to fight back!"

The auditorium erupts with movement.

The girl in the Student Council is set in motion, slicing through the restraints binding the students, and the liberated ones begin scrambling. The air pulses with the collective, feverish excitement of the students.

Rose knocks a man off his feet by releasing a surge of magic on him.

All for victory. That's what is on her mind.

At that moment, Rose realizes she is the symbol of their insurrection.

If she keeps fighting, they'll fight, too. She'll keep showing them an indisputable victory. Rose swings her sword at full power without focusing on how she's distributing magic in her body.

"Pursue the Student Council president!!"

"Swipe her sword!!"

She's the subject of attention and hate and applause as she slaughters multitudes of enemies and frees masses of students, all while continuing to fight.

Everyone admires and aspires to her valiancy.

But her combat style is also reckless, and she doesn't give her internal regulation of magic a second thought. Her power may be immense, but it's leaving her body, and she's rapidly approaching her limit. She can feel it as she calmly keeps an eye on her cap. Her magic is slipping away, causing her swordplay to dull as her body grows heavy.

One-hit kills become two hits, then three.

I'm almost done… Just a few more…, she thinks. But Rose can feel them closing in on her.

Just need to kill one more. She realizes something as she approaches her breaking point.

The zeal of the students has consumed the auditorium. Even if Rose is defeated, they won't stop fighting.

The boy has passed his wish on to Rose, who's distributed it to everyone. As countless lives are lost in battle, someone continues carrying his torch.

It hasn't been a waste.

His death—and the one that awaits her—haven't been for naught.

Rose from the kingdom of the arts has her reasons for studying the sword. She's never told anyone about them; it's nothing but a foolish dream she had as a child. And yet, it's a dream she chases earnestly. She hopes that she's come even slightly closer to actualizing it.

As those thoughts run through her mind, she takes her final swing.

It's nearly devoid of magic—not to mention weak and sluggish.

But she beheads the enemy with the most beautiful strike of her life.

It's the best sensation she's ever experienced. At that moment, she feels as if she's finally acquired a precious awareness of something.

And yet…it pains her to know she's achieved this when the end is nigh. Rose watches swords rain down on her from all sides, wishing she could live for just one more day.

And then it comes true.

An ebony whirlwind blasts through the enemies, causing them to spew gallons of blood and wiping them out in a flash.

Silence settles on the area, as if all time stands still.

In the eye of the hurricane stands a man wearing an ebony coat.

"Astounding. You're one who possesses beautiful swordplay…," he says to Rose in a voice that seems to echo from the depths of the earth.

He appears to be praising the way she handled her sword. His compliment affects her more than words can express.

"My name is Shadow."

The man who calls himself Shadow…is nothing short of frightening.

"I-I'm Rose. Rose Oriana…" Her voice trembles. She's too startled to rise to her feet.

His swordsmanship is far superior to hers. His abilities are the result of assiduous training, of eliminating excess, of honing, of integrating varied techniques. Rose feels as if time has ground down to a halt. She's never seen swordsmanship as flawless as this.

"Come to me… My loyal servants…"

Shadow releases magic with a blue-violet hue into the sky. As Rose bathes in that light, a group clad entirely in black drops into the auditorium.

Oh no, is this their backup…? Rose wonders.

But her fears are unfounded.

The team gracefully touches down and jumps into action.

This can't be an internal feud… But they also don't seem like they're from the Knight Order. Upon further inspection, she realizes the troop is comprised entirely of women. And on top of that…

"They're so strong…"

Every one of them is tough—a force of nature.

They chop down the captors in the blink of an eye.

The women possess the same sword techniques as Shadow. These fearless warriors are under his command.

"Master Shadow, I'm glad you're safe."

"Ah, Nu."

A woman clad in black approaches Shadow with a bow. "Their leader has torched the campus, fleeing the area."

"How pathetic… Leave him to me."

"Understood."

"Does he think he can escape…?" Shadow lets out a low chuckle.

Flinging his coat open, he slices open the auditorium doors with a single stroke of his sword. As an added bonus, the opponents in his vicinity become mounds of unmoving flesh.

He's slightly imitating Rose's swordsmanship, waving his weapon as if to flaunt it before calmly disappearing into the night.

Each of his movements sets a perfect example for Rose.

"Are you all right?" The girl known as Nu approaches her.

"Yes…"

"Those were some fantastic techniques," Nu comments, readying her ebony katana and leaping into the fight.

Her swordplay is extraordinary. She mows down the men in jet-black, leaving them facedown on the floor.

Rose can feel her common sense—no, her common sense as a dark knight—shattering into pieces. The swordsmanship exhibited by these warriors doesn't fit into any preexisting molds.

It's an entirely new art of its own.

Where did this powerful group and methodology come from? Rose is stunned she's never known of them until now.

"Fire! There's fire coming this way!"

The voice pulls Rose back to reality. She can see the flames rising in the back of the auditorium.

"Escape if you're near the exit!" Rose shouts, directing the students. Thanks to the all-women group, they can avoid needless sacrifices.

The end of the battle is near.

Rose escorts the wounded to the exit.

"The Knight Order is coming!!"

Everyone is relieved by that message. Rose releases the tension in her body and almost collapses but manages to pull herself together in a fluster.

The students are being evacuated from the auditorium one by one. The fire intensifies, and the men in black are exterminated.

Before Rose realizes it, the black-clad gang of women are gone.

They skillfully disappeared undetected, leaving no traces behind, as if they were never there at all.

Rose helps each student out of the auditorium until none remain and looks back at the overpowering flames that consume the structure.

"Who are they…?"

A distant blaze casts a faint glow over the assistant principal's office in the night.

A silhouette moves in the dark room, yanking several books off the shelves and letting them burn on the floor.

The books are consumed by the small fire that fiercely illuminates the room.

The figure is that of a scrawny man in jet-black.

"What're you doing dressed like that, Assistant Principal Lutheran…?"

The black shadow trembles. He should be the only one here, but a young boy managed to enter before he noticed.

The boy sits cross-legged on the sofa, reading a book. He's average-looking with black hair—a dime a dozen. But he doesn't even glance at the flames that spread from the shadow. His gaze is focused instead on a thick book. The sound of turning pages echoes throughout the room.

"How perceptive of you," notes the man, removing his mask to reveal a middle-aged face.

It is indeed Assistant Principal Lutheran, sporting gray streaks in his slicked-back hair.

Lutheran tosses his mask into the fire. Then he throws off his black clothes and incinerates them. The light intensifies.

"For my reference, I suppose you'll let me ask how you figured it out, Cid Kagenou."

Lutheran takes a seat across from the boy.

"I knew it the moment I saw you."

Cid glances up at Lutheran for a second before returning to his book.

"You knew just by looking at me, huh? Maybe it's the way I walk or my physique… Either way, you have a keen eye."

Lutheran glances at Cid, who's focused on his book.

Their two shadows quiver under the light of the flames.

"May I also ask you something for my reference?" Cid asks while staring at his book.

Lutheran silently urges him to proceed.

"Why did you do it? You don't seem the type who enjoys this kind of thing."

"Why? Well, it started long ago," mutters Lutheran, crossing his arms. "I was at the height of my career. Before you were even born."

"I've heard you won the Bushin Festival."

"Yes, but that's nowhere near my proudest moment. The height of my career was greater than that. You wouldn't understand if I told you."

Lutheran grins. He doesn't seem to be speaking facetiously but appears somewhat tired instead.

"Soon after I peaked, I fell terribly ill and was forced to retire. After years of struggle, all my honor instantly evaporated. As I was searching for a way to cure my illness, I found potential in an artifact researcher named Lukreia."

"I'm sorry. Is this story gonna take long?"

"A bit. Lukreia was Sherry's mother, an unfortunate woman hated by those in her field for being too smart for her own good. As a researcher, she possessed knowledge that was unmatched, and I found her beneficial to me. I supported her work and gathered artifacts for her, and she focused on her research, which I later used. She wasn't interested in fame or fortune, so we got along just fine. And then I stumbled upon the Eye of Avarice. It was the artifact for which I'd been searching. But you see, Lukreia...that stupid woman claimed it was unsafe, and she was about to request the nation store it for her. Which is why I killed her. After I cut her from her extremities inward, I impaled her heart and twisted my blade."

Cid's book remains open as he closes his eyes and listens to Lutheran's story.

"I acquired the Eye, but the research was incomplete. That's when I conveniently met another researcher—Sherry, Lukreia's daughter. She was naive and unknowing, catering to my every whim. She never knew I was the enemy, that sweet, stupid child. Thanks to mother and daughter, the Eye is now complete. All I had to do was set the stage to gather magic and prepare the perfect camouflage. Today...will be my greatest day, when all my dreams will come true."

Lutheran spitefully chortles to himself. "How's that for reference?"

In response, Cid cracks open his eyes. "I think I understood most of it. But...there's one thing I don't get."

"Try me."

"You said you killed Lukreia and used her daughter. Is that really true?" Cid shifts his eyes off the book and fixes his gaze on Lutheran.

"Of course it is. Does that anger you, Cid?"

"You'll never know... I can clearly separate what's important to me and what's not, you know." Cid slightly lowers his eyes.

"May I ask why?"

"I do it to stay focused. I have this one dream I always wanted to achieve, and it used to seem unattainable. Which is why I kept cutting things out of my life."

"Oh?"

"We all go through life amassing things we cherish. We acquire friends and lovers and jobs...and it keeps going from there. But on the other hand, I cut things out of my life. Deciding what I don't need. I've thrown so much away. At the end of the day, all that's left are the things I couldn't live without. That's all I live for, and I don't really care what happens otherwise."

Cid snaps the book closed. He rises to his feet and tosses it into the fire.

"You're telling me the fates of the foolish mother and daughter don't matter to you."

"No. I said I don't *really* care, but that doesn't mean I don't care at all. Right now, I feel slightly…disturbed." Cid brandishes the sword at his waist. "I think it's about time we start. Someone might barge in if we take too long."

"Yes. Sadly, we must part."

Two naked blades glisten in the flames, and the battle ends instantly.

Lutheran's sword pierces Cid's chest, which gushes with blood.

Cid crashes through the door, thrown into the blazing hallway. In a flash, his body is concealed by the crimson flames that engulf him.

"Farewell, young lad."

Lutheran withdraws his sword. The fire in the hallway has entered the room, becoming more intense, and he turns on his heels, about to leave the office.

"Where do you think you're going?"

"Nnr…!"

As if bouncing off the depths of an abyss, a deep voice resounds behind Lutheran. When he looks back, he finds a man in ebony wearing a magician's mask, a hood, and an ebony coat burning bright red. The newcomer pays no attention to the flames as he unveils his sword.

"Curse you…!" Lutheran readies his weapon.

"My name is Shadow. I lurk in the darkness and hunt down shadows…"

"So you're the one I've heard about…" Lutheran holds his naked sword steady.

Loosely gripping the hilt of his katana, Shadow confronts him.

The pair lock eyes for a moment. Lutheran is the first to look away.

"I see you're quite strong."

"Hmm..."

"I've also lived with my sword. I can understand almost everything once I confront my opponent...even the fact that I'm at a disadvantage right now. Sorry, but I must fight with all my might."

Lutheran retrieves a red pill from his breast pocket and swallows it before producing the Eye of Avarice and its command device.

"The Eye's true worth becomes apparent when the items are combined. Like this."

The two artifacts clank as they're joined, emitting a radiant light that forms into a helix of shining letters from an ancient alphabet. Lutheran laughs as he holds the artifacts to his chest.

"Here and now, I'll be reborn."

It sinks into his chest and clothes and skin, as if submerged into water.

"AAAAAAAAAaaaaaaaaaah!!" Lutheran roars as he claws at his chest.

The glowing ancient letters gather around him, engraving themselves into his body. A blinding luminescence dyes the room white.

Then the light dims, and Lutheran is found kneeling in white smoke.

He rises to his feet at a leisurely pace. When he looks forward, a series of small, glowing letters has been etched into his face like a tattoo.

"Fantastic... Incredible... My powers are returning, and my disease will be cured!"

Lutheran stands in the middle of a torpedo of flames that undulate under the force of his powerful magic. The glowing letters aren't just engraved in his face but also his hands and neck.

"You can never fathom my frenzied strength! This magic has far surpassed all human limitations!" Lutheran sneers.

"Let's try it out on you."

And then he vanishes.

The next moment, Lutheran takes a big swing at Shadow from

behind. There's a high-pitched echo, and the air between them ripples from impact.

"Oh, impressive parry."

Upon inspection, Shadow has blocked the attack with his ebony blade as he continues facing forward. Lutheran uses all his might to grind against it, but his opponent's weapon won't budge.

"I underestimated you. But how's this?"

Lutheran disappears again.

This time, there are shrill noises in succession.

One, two, three.

Every time, Shadow's blade adjusts slightly, his movement as minimal as possible.

On the fourth, Lutheran appears before him.

"I didn't think you would block that one. I acknowledge your strength." He stares at Shadow and grins calmly.

"To properly respect it, I'll now unveil my true power." Lutheran shifts his stance.

He focuses a devastating amount of magic on the sword raised above his head.

"In the afterlife, you can pride yourself on making me unleash my might."

That single blow comes at Shadow with the power and speed to crush him into smithereens.

But the ebony blade parries it with ease.

"What?!"

A burst of sparks flies between the black blade and the sword of light.

"You dare block that, too?!"

"At your level…I'd hope so."

The two glare at each other from a dangerously close distance.

"Ksh… I've only just begun!"

Lutheran's sword slashes rapidly, leaving behind a beautiful trajectory of white afterimages in the air.

"RAAAAaaaah!!"

As Lutheran roars, the ebony blade repels all his attacks.

"AAAAAaauugh!!"

The white strikes slam into the ebony blade, the two crashing loudly together as if composing a song. It adds another layer to the burning night.

But that's about to end.

With one swipe of the ebony blade, Lutheran is flung backward, crashing into the desks and tumbling to the floor.

"Gak… Impossible…!"

Lutheran clutches his stinging body as he gets to his feet. His wounds will heal quickly, but it looks as if the ancient text is growing dim.

"I didn't think this would be a struggle. Heh, I'm impressed. But no matter how strong you are, I'll end all of you."

"What do you mean…?"

"Well, I've arranged for the incidents to look like they're the work of the Shadow Garden. From the evidence to the testimonies—everything has been prepared. Regardless of your strength in battle, you'll only suffer in the end."

Lutheran chortles, screwing up his face before observing Shadow's response.

But Shadow is laughing. A dreadfully deep guffaw spills out of him.

"What's so funny?"

"It's amusing how you think something this insignificant could end us."

Lutheran stops smiling. "You're just afraid to admit defeat."

Shadow shakes his head as if to say, *You don't know a thing*.

"From the beginning, we've walked the path of neither justice nor evil. We walk our own path."

Shadow holds out his burning ebony coat.

"You talk big. Accuse us for the sins of the world. We'll accept them as our own, but nothing will change. We'll still do what we're meant to do."

"You say you don't fear opposing the world? Mighty arrogant of you, Shadow!"

"Then crush it out of me."

Lutheran lunges, his bare sword swinging down on Shadow from overhead.

But Shadow evades the attack, right before his head is split in two.

"What?!"

There's a spray of fresh blood.

The ebony blade has been thrust into Lutheran's right wrist, and he immediately switches his sword in his left hand and starts retreating.

"Impossible!"

This time, the black sword slices through his left wrist. While Lutheran falls back, Shadow's katana plunges toward him.

"Guh…gah…!"

Lutheran is soiled with his own blood as he fails to counter the swift slashes that his eyes can't even perceive. His wrists, feet, upper arms, and thighs are stabbed hundreds of times.

The next series of attacks concentrate on his core.

"Cut from your extremities inward…"

Shadow's deep voice echoes between each stab.

"…And twist my blade in your heart, I believe?" he confirms, plunging his blade into Lutheran's chest at the same time.

"Wha—…?!!"

Even as blood gushes into his mouth, Lutheran grabs the weapon wedged in his heart and resists. His eyes meet the boy's gaze from behind his mask.

"It can't be. You're Ci—…!"

The moment he's about to finish his sentence, the blade twists.

"Ga…agh…aghh…!"

When it's yanked out, a river of blood pumps from his chest. The light in Lutheran's eyes and the ancient text begin to fade. All that remains is the corpse of a gaunt, middle-aged man.

And then there's the quiet pattering of footsteps.

"Foster Father…?"

Head to toe in splattered blood, Shadow whips around to see…a girl with peach hair.

"Foster Fatherrrr!!" She sprints past Shadow and cradles the corpse.

"No… How…? Why…?!!"

She clings to the gaunt body and weeps. Her foster father moves no more. Shadow watches her tears fall and wet the corpse's face before turning away.

"It's better you don't know…"

And then he disappears into the madder-red flames, leaving her cries behind him.

She hears that the boy with a major back injury is being protected at school.

When the news reaches Rose, she can't help but hurry to the first aid tent at the school that burns in the darkness of the night.

Students and instructors with hands to spare assist with a bucket brigade.

The Knight Order makes moves to treat the injured and track down the Shadow Garden.

And Rose finally arrives at the tent after maneuvering through the flustered crowd.

The boy in treatment is a first-year dark knight with black hair, and he has the same features as the one for whom she's searching.

But he should've died back there—though it wasn't like she checked his vital signs. She hadn't had the time or composure for that.

Which means maybe—just maybe—he could be alive. He could be the one inside that tent.

Rose can't abandon that faint glimmer of hope.

Her mind negates the prospect while her heart hopes it's true. Rose notices how weak this is making her.

Inside the tent reeks of blood and alcohol. The first aid team are in a rush, busily attending to patients. Rose makes her way through the tent, checking each face—until she finds the boy with black hair.

He's lying facedown on a bed, being treated for his back wound.

The doctor is talking to him.

He's conscious...maybe.

"U-ummm... Are you Cid Kagenou?" Rose sounds as if she wants to ask a favor.

"Yes...?" He twists around to look at her. It's the face of that same heroic boy.

"I'm glad...so glad..."

"Wait...huh?!"

At some point, she's embraced Cid, clinging to him tightly as his head squirms against her breast. Rose vows to never lose him again.

Something hot rises to her chest.

"Um... We're in the middle of treatment..."

"Oh! Right."

The timid voice of the doctor snaps Rose out of her daze, and she releases Cid.

"And how are his wounds?"

"The gash on his back is deep. It's a miracle it didn't damage his nerves or internal organs. It's not fatal."

"Oh my gosh! Really?!"

"Yes, really."

"Wow! That's great!" Her entire body quivers with joy.

"Um, yeah, so I think I unconsciously dodged a fatal attack. No, I was passed out, so I don't really know, but that's how I survived." Cid sounds defensive for some unfathomable reason.

"You must have acted on reflex, thanks to your persistent training. Amazing."

"Um, not exactly."

Rose kneels before him and looks into his eyes. "No, that's it. Your undying efforts and passion gave life to this miracle."

She caresses Cid's cheek as she gazes at him, standing close enough for him to almost feel her breath.

"Um..."

"You don't have to say anything. I absolutely accept your feelings."

Her eyes well up with tears as she peers at him, and her cheeks turn as red as a rose.

"That's fine if you're convinced I miraculously survived. But don't go saying it was some strange anomaly afterward."

"All right. For now, please get some rest."

"Negotiation complete. Good night."

Rose fondly watches him close his eyes and fall asleep. Her heart has never raced so fast in her life.

Bu-dump, bu-dump, it throbs.

Up until this point, she's only heard tell of this feeling, but now she's finally experiencing it firsthand.

"Since you've saved my life...I shall give my heart to you..."

She strokes Cid's hair and stays by his side until dawn.

"Don't you think they did a good job?" asks an alarmingly attractive blond elf, presenting a sheet of paper.

In an ebony dress that makes her look like darkness itself, she's in the Mitsugoshi building late at night.

Gamma takes the paper from the beauty and mumbles, "Lady Alpha... Um, I don't know what to say."

"I'm sorry. It's a tough question to answer."

Alpha snickers to herself. The paper she handed over is a wanted poster containing a sketch of Shadow in his ebony coat.

"SHADOW: ENEMY OF THE ROYAL KINGDOM. WANTED FOR MASS MURDER, ARSON, THEFT, KIDNAPPING... What a naughty man."

"You're also on the wanted poster for the Shadow Garden, Lady Alpha. Though it only mentions your name."

"Where?"

Gamma takes out another paper for Alpha to read.

"The Shadow Garden… What a horrible organization."

The glow of the fireplace lights up her profile, and her supernatural beauty radiates from the darkness.

"But it's a shame. I can't believe we rushed back here to find it almost over."

Alpha tosses the wanted poster into the fire, muttering to herself as she watches the flames lap it up and black char creep onto the edges of the paper.

"Accuse us for the sins of the world. We'll accept them as our own, but nothing will change. We'll still do what we're meant to do. How beautiful…"

Alpha watches the poster turn to ash.

"Deep down, I used to think I stood on the side of justice. But he wasn't like that."

The light and shadows across her alluring face shift with the swaying flames. At times, she has the looks of a goddess, and at others, a devil. The fire capriciously switches between the two.

"He's prepared, and we must follow suit."

Alpha turns back to Gamma, who nervously gulps upon seeing her face.

"Gather every available member of the Seven Shadows."

"I will. Right away." Gamma bows her head. Cold sweat trails down her neck and vanishes between her breasts.

After a chilly evening wind blows by her, Gamma lifts her head. There's no one there.

All that's left is the flames in the fireplace flickering violently.

"Excuse me…!"

Hearing someone call out to him in front of the half-charred campus, the ordinary boy with black hair turns.

"Oh, sorry about that. I was totally spacing out. What's up?"

"I heard I might be able to meet you if I waited here. There's something I want to talk to you about...," admits a girl with peach hair, gazing at him.

"Sure. It'll be a while before the authorities question me anyway. Plus, classes are gonna be canceled for a while."

"Um...thank you for the other day." She lightly bows her head. "You really saved me, Cid."

"It was nothing."

"I couldn't have done it without you."

"It's all good. Don't worry about it."

"Also, there's something else I have to tell you. Um, I've decided to study abroad."

"Oh, that explains all that luggage."

There are heaps upon heaps of bags around her.

"Yes. I'll be taking a carriage to Laugus."

"So you're going to the college town... Wow, that's great."

"There's something I must do. I have to go because I can't do it with the knowledge I have now."

"All right. I wish you the best."

"And because...there's no longer a reason for me to be here." She mournfully turns back to the school. "I wish we could've talked more, Cid..."

"Me too. But we'll meet again someday."

"Yeah, I look forward to it." She grins and walks past him.

"Oh, wait a sec."

"Yes?" She halts at the sound of his voice and turns.

"Can I ask what it is you have to do?"

The girl smiles uneasily. "It's a secret."

"I see."

"But when it's all over...will you listen to my story?"

"...Sure."

The pair grin before walking away from each other.

As they part, the billowing clouds overhead block the summer sun, and the lukewarm breeze carries the scent of rain.

"I promise to..."

And the wind carries her whisper to his ears.

He seems to have heard the entire sentiment—a string of words unintended for his ears. He turns to look back at her as she gets smaller and smaller, farther and farther away from him.

Small raindrops drip down from the sky, moistening her light-pink hair, and he continues walking as if nothing happened.

And neither turns back again.

Appendix

“Even side characters have their own battles to fight.”

Cid Kagenou

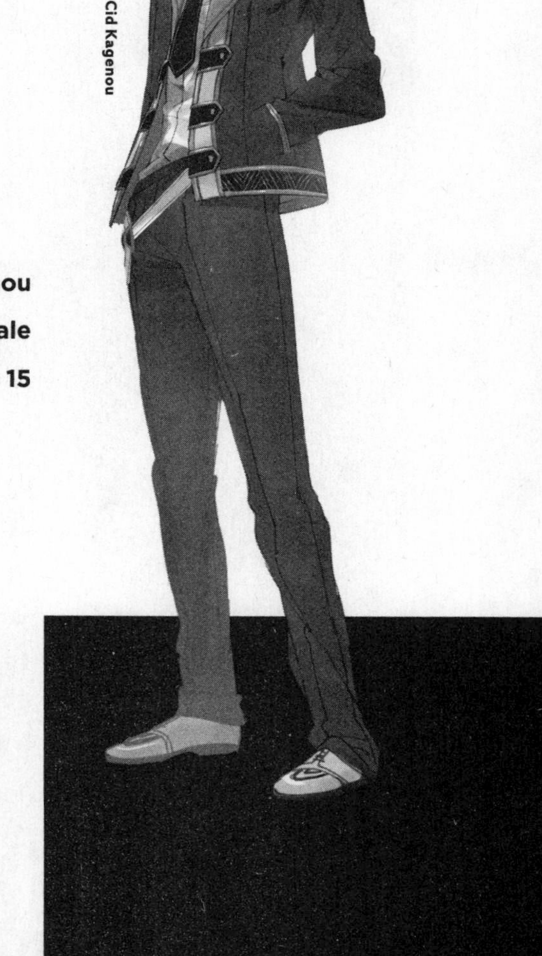

Name: Cid Kagenou

Gender: Male

Age: 15

A young boy who endured extreme training to become a shadowbroker and reincarnated in another world following a tragic accident. Currently fighting to make his broken dreams from his past life come true. The founder of the underground organization the Shadow Garden...which he doesn't do much to rule or control. All he wants to do is to pretend he's Shadow and play mastermind.

Alpha

Name: Alpha

Gender: Female

Age: 15

"If that's what you want, then I'll devote my life to it..."

A young elven girl resurrected from a mound of rotting flesh with Cid's healing methods (*cough*, experiment, *cough*). Endlessly grateful to Cid for saving her life and devotes herself to him. The honorable first member of Shadow Garden and the first seat in Seven Shadows. Basically rules the organization, since Cid won't do anything. Too competent for her own good, causing the organization to expand at an alarming rate.

Alexia Midgar

"Good boy, Pooch. Now fetch!"

Name: Alexia Midgar

Gender: Female

Age: 15

A princess of the Midgar Kingdom. In the same grade as Cid at the Midgar Academy for Dark Knights. Outwardly pretends to have a gentle disposition but is actually a sadistic princess who makes Cid her personal pet. Grew up always compared to her brilliant older sister. Still has a complex about it. Doesn't exactly hate Cid but has trouble being honest with him.

Sherry Barnett

Name: Sherry Barnett

Gender: Female

Age: 16

= Sherry Barnett

"When it's all over, will you listen to my story?"

A student at the Midgar Academy of Science and foster child of the assistant principal. Dives into researching artifacts to cope after watching her mother get murdered when she was a child. One of the greatest researchers in the nation. Her foster father worries that she has no friends at school. Bad at everything but research.

The Chronicles of Master Shadow Complete Version: Volume 1

By Beta

To lurk in the darkness and hunt down shadows. That's the path Master Shadow has chosen. That's why the fruits of his labor will stay hidden in the shadows and forgotten without recognition.

It doesn't matter what evil he slays, how many things he protects, or if he saves the world—no one will praise him. This is the path Master Shadow has chosen.

Which is why I'll write about his battles, his beliefs, his journey...in hopes that the world will someday acknowledge and reward him.

When Master Shadow was a child, he learned the truth about the Cult of Diablos and trained for years to defeat the powerful enemy himself. After training endlessly, he finally acquired great power and shadow intelligence.

But I wonder how much he had to sacrifice in return. To lose one's childhood dreams and happy future. To throw away friends and family and lovers and everything else. It must have been a hellish road to travel... He sacrificed his happiness to save others. That's how Master Shadow saved me. He's given those of us who were shunned for being possessed, who were left to die on the edge of hopelessness, a new lease on life.

We decided to fight the Cult of Diablos and want to do anything we can to assist Master Shadow. We believe that the downfall of this cult will grant him true happiness…

[Contents Omitted]

And now, I will relate two of Master Shadow's earliest battles.

The first incident happened when a member of the royal family was kidnapped by the wicked Cult of Diablos to resurrect the power of Diablos the demon. The victim was a beautiful princess with silver hair and a cry[illegible] and then Master Shadow came to the rescue of the princess!

He gallantly appeared on the scene right when the beautiful princess was in danger and slayed the Cult's assassin, Zenon. Even though the man was the greatest fencing instructor in the country, he couldn't lay a hand on Master Shadow. That's the extent of our leader's frightening power.

Master Shadow brought out the greatest esoteric technique to exterminate that numbskull Zenon. That one strike colored the sky, blew away the rain clouds, and Master Shadow's almighty majesty was shown to the entire world!

The second incident was when Lutheran, a former member of the Rounds in the Cult of Diablos, foolishly attacked

Master Shadow's school. Lutheran used an artifact to seal the magic of all his students, but that would obviously *never* stop Master Shadow! While the students were taken hostage, Master Shadow plucked off the terrorists from the shadows, one by one.

Using his shadow wisdom, Master Shadow had no trouble freeing the magic sealed in the artifact. I bet Lutheran tipped his hat to him for that heroic deed. They say it's not his overwhelming might that makes him scary—but his brain. After freeing the hostages, Master Shadow ambushed the ringleader of the operation who tried to flee and destroyed his sinister ambitions. And he bore the burden of Lutheran's sins, choosing to save a girl on his own...

All right...that's where I'll leave off for Volume 1. There aren't enough pages to describe his splendid battles.

But rest assured, I promise to log two more in Volume 2.

In the next installment, we'll discover if a guard to the sanctuary actually dares to block Master Shadow!

Upon sneaking into a sanctuary to unravel the mystery of Diablos the demon, Aurora the Calamity Witch appears before him. As they proceed through the sanctuary together, there's someone blocking their path: the hero who fought the demon in the past! What might await them at the end of their battle?!

And we'll also uncover what malice lurks around the Bushin Festival!

Master Shadow takes the stage at the Bushin Festival as he hides his true identity. What could his motives be...? Will Master Shadow clash with the Cult of Diablos as he pulls the strings behind the scenes?! And at the end of his fight, what will he think? ...Who will he rescue?!

A must-see for die-hard Master Shadow fans!! Bear witness to this spectacular double feature of his outstanding feats!!

And stay tuned for the complete version of the *Chronicles of Master Shadow* in Volume 2!!

Afterword

Thank you for reading Volume 1 of *The Eminence in Shadow.*

This book is a novelization of a web series that I uploaded called *Shousetsuka ni Narou*. Even though I initially submitted the series just for fun, I started to think *Maybe I'll take a break after I'm done with the first chapter*...after I received virtually no response to it. But shortly thereafter, my story started climbing the rankings, and it drastically changed the fate of this book.

And that led to a lot of people reading my work and giving me their thoughts, which brought me joy and made me think, *I want to write more!* Then, thanks to all your support, I was asked to novelize the series as I was writing it, and now it's published in the form of this first volume. My novel was lost in the sea of stories online, but thanks to you, all the readers who supported my work, my story has become a book. Thank you so much.

Now that I'm in a position where I get to write my own afterword, I've realized that I've never properly read one before. I wonder how many people who read this entire book will also read this. This is just my own estimate, but I'm guessing less than 10 percent. But I know that 10 percent definitely found my book interesting. I mean, if they're willing to read the afterword, they must have! And that's a fact!

Which brings me to you, the dear reader who's read all the way up to this point! Hey, you! I have a favor to ask you!

Would you mind telling other people about this book? It can be your pals at school, your colleagues, your Internet chums, or people who share the same interests. The publishing industry seems to have hit a slump, and my novel is no exception! It's barely hanging in there! My next book is gonna be really exciting, so it would mean a lot if I could have your support. If all readers were to spread the word, it would really help bring my book to different audiences. Even saying *I'd recommend this book* would be great! I hope it isn't too much trouble!

I'm going to end here, but before that, I'd like to thank my editor, who helped me when I didn't know squat about the publishing world. And I extend my gratitude to Touzai for the best illustrations I could ever hope for, to Araki at BALCOLONY. for the incredible designs that color this book, and to all my readers for their support. Thank you again from the bottom of my heart.

Let's meet again in Volume 2!

Daisuke Aizawa

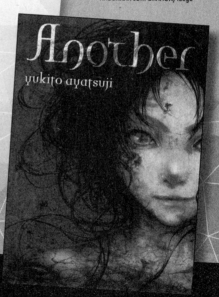